EinFach Englisch
Unterrichtsmodell

Nick McDonell

Twelve

Edited by
Hannes Pfeiffer

Series Editor:
Hans Kröger

Vorwort

Einzelarbeit

Partnerarbeit

Gruppenarbeit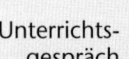

Unterrichtsgespräch

Schreibauftrag

Hausaufgabe

filmische Präsentation

Projekt, offene Aufgabe

kreative Aufgabe

szenisches Spiel, Rollenspiel

Der Titel der Reihe **EinFach Englisch** verdeutlicht Zielsetzung und Programm zugleich. Einerseits soll Schülerinnen und Schülern auf einfache Art und Weise der Zugang zu klassischen, aber auch neuen literarischen Werken und Filmen ermöglicht werden, andererseits sollen Lehrerinnen und Lehrern in der Praxis erprobte Unterrichtsmodelle angeboten werden, die die wichtigsten methodisch-didaktischen Ansätze ihres Faches Englisch abdecken. Dabei sind die Modelle direkt, ohne langes Einlesen einsetzbar und stellen Unterrichtsarbeit konkret vor. Als besonders hilfreich für die Praxis haben sich dabei folgende Aspekte erwiesen, die für die Gestaltung der Reihe wesentlich sind:

- Überblick über **Figurenkonstellation**, ggf. **Filmszenen** und **Inhalt**
- **Klausuren** mit **Erwartungshorizont**
- **Arbeitsblätter**, **Tafelbilder** und **Leitfragen** für den Unterricht
- **Piktogramme** als Hinweise auf **Unterrichts-** und **Arbeitsformen**

Das Prinzip der „**Components**" ermöglicht darüber hinaus den variablen Einsatz der Modelle in unterschiedlich konzipierten Unterrichtsreihen. Dabei stehen Machbarkeit und Praxisnähe stets im Vordergrund.

Das vorliegende Modell bezieht sich auf folgende Textausgabe:
Nick McDonell, *Twelve*, © Philipp Reclam jun. GmbH & Co., Stuttgart 2005
ISBN 978-3-15-009127-2

Sprachliche Betreuung: Elin Arbin

© 2010 Bildungshaus Schulbuchverlage
Westermann Schroedel Diesterweg Schöningh Winklers GmbH
Braunschweig, Paderborn, Darmstadt

www.schoeningh-schulbuch.de
Schöningh Verlag, Jühenplatz 1–3, 33098 Paderborn

Das Werk und seine Teile sind urheberrechtlich geschützt.
Jede Nutzung in anderen als den gesetzlich zugelassenen Fällen bedarf der
vorherigen schriftlichen Einwilligung des Verlages.
Hinweis zu § 52a UrhG: Weder das Werk noch seine Teile dürfen ohne eine
solche Einwilligung gescannt und in ein Netzwerk gestellt werden.
Das gilt auch für Intranets von Schulen und sonstigen Bildungseinrichtungen.

Auf verschiedenen Seiten dieses Buches befinden sich Verweise (Links) auf
Internetadressen. Haftungshinweis: Trotz sorgfältiger inhaltlicher Kontrolle wird
die Haftung für die Inhalte der externen Seiten ausgeschlossen. Für den Inhalt
dieser externen Seiten sind ausschließlich deren Betreiber verantwortlich. Sollten
Sie dabei auf kostenpflichtige, illegale oder anstößige Inhalte treffen, so bedauern
wir dies ausdrücklich und bitten Sie, uns umgehend per E-Mail davon in Kenntnis
zu setzen, damit beim Nachdruck der Verweis gelöscht wird.

Druck 5 4 3 2 1 / Jahr 2014 13 12 11 10
Die letzte Zahl bezeichnet das Jahr dieses Druckes.

Umschlaggestaltung: Jennifer Kirchhof
Druck und Bindung: Media-Print Informationstechnologie GmbH, Paderborn

ISBN 978-3-14-041194-3

Getting started

Can we please all stand and have a moment of silence for those students who died.

And can we now have a moment of silence for those students who killed them.

Nick McDonell: *Twelve*, © Philipp Reclam jun. GmbH & Co., Stuttgart 2005, p. 4

What might the circumstances of these deaths have been?
Who could have said these words?

Nick McDonell: *Twelve*

1. Die Personen **6**
2. Der Inhalt **8**
3. The author **14**
4. Vorüberlegungen zum Einsatz des Romans im Unterricht **15**
5. Klausuren **16**
6. Konzeption des Unterrichtsmodells **22**
7. Components **24**
8. Further reading **100**

Component 1: Sparking curiosity 24

1.1 Writing a novel at 17!? **24**
1.2 Creating atmosphere **24**
 ■ Copy 1: The Upper East Side in Manhattan/Private boarding schools in the USA **26**
1.3 Getting to know White Mike **27**
 ■ Copy 2: White Mike **29**
 ■ Copy 3: Talking about characters – Some important facts **30**

Component 2: Part I (pp. 5–48) – Getting to know the characters – and the book 31

2.1 Who else is hanging around the Upper East Side? **31**
 ■ Copy 4: Introducing some characters in *Twelve* **32**
 ■ Copy 5: Some kid I met in New York **33**
 ■ Copy 6: The kid we met **35**
 ■ Copy 7: The American school system **37**
2.2 A look back at part I **38**
 ■ Copy 8: Looking back at part I **39**
 ■ Copy 8a: Looking back at part I (solutions) **40**
 ■ Copy 9: Streetmap of the Upper East Side **41**
2.3 The point of view **42**
2.4 Rounding off **42**

Component 3: Part II (pp. 49–96) – Rising action 44

3.1 The action rises – getting into part II **44**
 ■ Copy 10: Part II – Rising action **45**
 ■ Copy 10a: Part II – Rising action (solutions) **46**
3.2 "I'm not a slut!" – Sara's plan to become famous **47**
3.3 White Mike – The linchpin of the plot **48**
3.4 Jessica – the drug victim **49**
 ■ Copy 11: Drugs in Nick McDonell's *Twelve* **50**
 ■ Copy 11a: Drugs in Nick McDonell's *Twelve* (solutions) **51**
 ■ Copy 12: Drug abuse and drug prevention **53**

Component 4: Music and language in *Twelve* 54

- 4.1 The songs in parts I and II 54
  - Copy 13: James Taylor: *Fire and rain* 57
  - Copy 14: Nelly: *Ride wit me* 58
  - Copy 15: Ben Harper: *Burn one down* 59
- 4.2 Parental advisory – explicit language! 60
  - Copy 16: Colloquial and explicit language in *Twelve* 62
  - Copy 16a: Colloquial and explicit language in *Twelve* (solutions) 63
  - Copy 17: Study vocab part I 64
  - Copy 18: Study vocab part II 65
  - Copy 19: Study vocab "Songs and singers" 66
  - Copy 20: Study vocab part III 67
  - Copy 21: Study vocab part IV 68
  - Copy 22: Study vocab part V 69

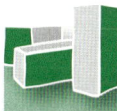

Component 5: Part III (pp. 97–121) – The action slows down 70

- 5.1 It's Sunday in New York City 70
- 5.2 What's your passion? 72
- 5.3 White Mike's Sunday – "How weird is this?" 73
  - Copy 23: White Mike's growing discomfort with his job 76
  - Copy 23a: White Mike's growing discomfort with his job (solutions) 77

Component 6: Part IV (pp. 123–172) – Complex relationships 78

- 6.1 Strangers: Parents and kids in *Twelve* 78
  - Copy 24: Looking back at part IV 79
  - Copy 24a: Looking back at part IV (solutions) 80
  - Copy 25: Role cards 82
  - Copy 26: The kids and their parents – a written discussion 83
- 6.2 White Mike – the center of the novel 84
  - Copy 27: White Mike 87
  - Copy 27a: White Mike (solutions) 88

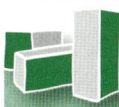

Component 7: Part V (pp. 173–221) and post-reading activities 89

- 7.1 The party – a massacre 89
- 7.2 Part V – It's like a movie 91
  - Copy 28: Field sizes 92
  - Copy 29: A film scene 94
- 7.3 White Mike's characterization 95
  - Copy 30: White Mike's characterization 97
- 7.4 The butterfly effect and *Twelve* 98
  - Copy 31: Cause and effect – the butterfly effect in *Twelve* 99
- 7.5 More ideas for post-reading activities 100

Die Personen

White Mike

Er ist die Hauptperson, der Dreh- und Angelpunkt des Romans. Er ist Teil aller Handlungsstränge, die am Ende auf der Silvesterparty zusammengeführt werden.

Zugleich ist er auch die rundeste Figur, da der Leser von ihm am meisten erfährt: zum einen, weil er in jedem Handlungsstrang vorkommt, zum anderen, weil Nick McDonell ihm viele Rückblenden gewidmet hat, die von seiner Vergangenheit berichten.

White Mike zieht es vor, nach der High School ein Jahr zu pausieren, und verdient seinen Lebensunterhalt als Drogendealer. Umso erstaunlicher ist es, dass er selbst noch nie Drogen, weder legale noch illegale, zu sich genommen hat. Seit einigen Jahren ist Mike Halbwaise und lebt bei seinem Vater, der sich jedoch nicht um ihn kümmert. Im Laufe des Romans hegt White Mike immer größere Zweifel an seinem Tun und ist besorgt über den Hedonismus unter seinen Altersgenossen (den er mit seinen Drogen natürlich unterstützt!). Als er gegen Ende des Romans erfährt, dass sein Cousin Charlie von einem anderen Dealer, Lionel, erschossen wurde, rastet er aus und geht auf Lionel los. Dieser schießt auf Mike und löst dadurch das finale Massaker aus.

Sara

Sara ist das schönste Mädchen der Upper East Side und entsprechend bekannt. Das genügt ihr allerdings nicht. Sie möchte berühmt werden und sich durch die Silvesterparty ein Denkmal setzen. Geschickt setzt sie ihren Sexappeal ein, um Chris dazu zu überreden, eine zweite Party zu geben, weil ihre Eltern zu Hause sind, Chris hingegen „sturmfreie Bude" hat. Schließlich bekommt sie ihre große Party, schon früh sind über 50 Gäste da. „Legendär" wird die Party leider nur wegen des Massakers, das sie jedoch überlebt.

Chris

Der 17-jährige Chris ist auf der Suche nach sich selbst und nach dem ersten Sex. Durch privaten Boxunterricht versucht er, selbstbewusster zu werden. Geld spielt bei ihm keine Rolle, es ist im Überfluss da. Sein Elternhaus ist voll mit teurem Mobiliar und technischen Geräten. Seine Eltern sind weg, so lässt er sich überreden, eine große Silvesterparty zu geben – in der Hoffnung, Sara, den Traum aller Jungen, zu bekommen. Auf der Party versucht er noch, White Mike daran zu hindern, Lionel zu finden, kann den Lauf der Dinge jedoch nicht mehr aufhalten.

Jessica

Auch Jessica kommt aus reichem Hause. Obwohl noch minderjährig, hat sie sich bereits ihre Nase richten lassen. Insgesamt ist sie hübsch, sportlich und vor allem sehr intelligent. Schon vor dem High School Abschluss hat sie eine Zusage vom Wesleyan College, einer ebenso renommierten wie teuren Universität, bekommen. Im Laufe des Buches verfällt Jessica der Designerdroge „Twelve" und bietet schließlich an, mit dem Dealer Lionel zu schlafen, um an mehr „Twelve" zu gelangen.

Die Personen

Claude

Chris' Bruder Claude ist eine geheimnisvolle Figur. Meist hält er sich in seinem verdunkelten Zimmer auf und beschäftigt sich mit seiner Waffensammlung, die er in einer Art Schrein verwahrt. Er ist bekannt in der Upper East Side, da er schwer kokainabhängig war und bereits eine Entziehungskur hinter sich hat. Er zieht sich immer mehr in sein Zimmer zurück, und sein Faible für Waffen sowie der Überfluss an Geld führen schließlich dazu, dass er sich eine Uzi kauft, mit der er dann auf Chris' Party ein Massaker anrichtet und acht Menschen tötet. Er selbst wird von der Polizei erschossen.

Andrew

Ähnlich wie Chris ist auch Andrew ein „Opfer" Saras. Widerwillig kauft er Marihuana bei White Mike, um Sara zu gefallen. Er ist ein ruhiger Typ, der nicht oft auf Partys geht. Auf der Silvesterparty bahnt sich gerade ein Flirt mit Molly an, der jedoch durch Claudes Amoklauf jäh beendet wird. Wie Molly wird auch Andrew erschossen.

Nebenfiguren

Hunter und **Nana** tauchen früh im Roman auf. Hunter ist ein guter Freund von White Mike, der unter Mordverdacht gerät, weil er in eine Schlägerei mit Nana verwickelt war, bevor dieser zusammen mit White Mikes Cousin Charlie von Lionel erschossen wird.
Lionel dealt mit „Twelve" und wird somit zur wichtigsten Person für Jessica, die sich ihm anbietet, um mehr Drogen zu bekommen. Lionel taucht nicht oft auf; dadurch, dass er Charlie erschossen hat und schließlich auch auf White Mike schießt, löst er das Massaker mit aus.
Molly ist eine Freundin von White Mike. Sie ist die Einzige, die nichts davon weiß, dass Mike ein Dealer ist. Sie ist Model und eigentlich nicht gerne auf Partys. Allerdings hat sie eine Verabredung mit einem anderen Model, Tobias, und geht schließlich doch auf die Party. Molly ist eines der Opfer von Claude.
Timmy und Mark Rothko sind zwei Weiße, die den Stil von Gangsterrappern nachahmen und sich so total lächerlich machen. Ihre Funktion ist die des „comic relief". Beide werden von Claude erschossen.

Der Inhalt

White Mike is one of the rich kids in the Upper East Side in Manhattan. He takes a year off after high school and spends his time dealing drugs. All the young people are bored and long for shallow pleasures, such as sex and drugs. The novel covers five days, from December 27 to New Year's Eve, and tells the story of White Mike and his peers.
A shocking story about privileged and spoiled teenagers who do not know how privileged they are.

Part I – Friday, December 27		
Ch.	Contents	Comments
1	Introduction of White Mike, first *flashback* ("He had been awake for three days").	p. 9, l. 11 f.: Mike's mother is dead.
2	Hunter at the Rec., fight with Nana.	p. 13, l. 10 ff.: first scene that is like a movie
3	White Mike and Hunter at Rec. and McDonald's, their relationship is established, colleges and future are discussed.	
4	*Flashback: The Plague* mentioned for the first time, further characterization of White Mike.	Literature: *The Plague* (Albert Camus); whole chapter in *italics*
5	Hunter at home, alienation from parents who are rich yet unhappy.	Song: *Fire and Rain* (James Taylor)
6	Nana and white kid (who later turns out to be White Mike's cousin Charlie) get shot; setting (the projects) as juxtaposition to Hunter's neighbourhood.	Killer has "yellow blood-shot eyes" → Lionel as described on p. 67
7	Enter Sara Ludlow, her vanity and shallowness are introduced.	
8	NYC – the capital of the world, White Mike reflects on materialism and greed in NYC.	Song: *Ride wit me* (Nelly)
9	Enter Chris, description of his complexes, first party: Sara's plan for a bigger party at Chris's place starts to develop.	Song: *Burn One Down* (Ben Harper)
10	Enter Jessica, her first contact with "Twelve".	Gettysburg Address mentioned
11	Sara: Chris "might be useful".	
12	Enter Claude and Tobias, main focus on Claude, no closer description of Tobias; they are on a shopping spree for weapons in Chinatown.	One of the longest chapters in the novel
13	White Mike's report card.	Literature: *Shogun, Nietzsche*
14	Chris finds Jessica passed out in bathroom.	
15	*Flashback:* White Mike reflects on city life again, story of a rapist scaring a schoolmate of White Mike's.	Whole chapter in *italics*

| \multicolumn{3}{c}{**Part II – Saturday, December 28**} |
Ch.	Contents	Comments
16	Hunter is arrested.	
17	*Flashback:* White Mike, Hunter, Warren and Charlie at the zoo with their nanny. Kids did not respect her, now White Mike appreciates her efforts.	Whole chapter in *italics*
18	Ice-skating scene. Shallowness of Sara and her friends is emphasized. Andrew gets hurt by Jessica's skate. Andrew originally wanted to meet Hunter, but can't as Hunter is in jail.	
19	Jessica calls Chris to get White Mike's number.	
20	Andrew meets Sara in hospital.	Music: *Under the Table and Dreaming* (Dave Matthew's Band)
21	*Flashback:* White Mike's first night in his new room.	We learn that Mike's mother died of breast cancer. Whole chapter in *italics*.
22	Sara at Chris's. Sara establishes her plan of having a great party that will make her famous.	Song: *California Love* (Tupac Shakur)
23	White Mike and Lionel sell Twelve to Jessica. Mike is concerned about the drug and knows that it will do her no good.	Lionel mentioned for the first time. "Yellow bloodshot eyes" hints at him being Nana's murderer (cf. p. 24).
24	*Flashback:* White Mike in the dark kitchen.	
25	White Mike and Lionel continued: Lionel's thoughts identify him as Charlie's murderer.	We know more than White Mike about his cousin Charlie! When will he find out?
26	Jessica walks away from the deal.	
27	*Flashback:* Hunter asks White Mike why he doesn't do drugs. "I just never had the urge to."	Whole chapter in *italics*
28	White Mike remembers Charlie pawning his mother's necklace and buying the gun he later points at Lionel. *Flashback:* White Mike tells Charlie that it's not about how fast you pull your gun but how fast you pull the trigger, which is actually why Charlie is killed in ch. 6.	Song: *Ride wit me* (Nelly)
29	Tobias in the agency. He is extremely vain.	
30	Enter Molly. Also a model, but the opposite of Tobias. *Flashback:* Molly and White Mike in the Bahamas.	Literature: *Ragtime*
31	Tobias and Molly at Claude's to watch the piranhas. Molly does not fit into Tobias's world.	
32	Hunter in jail thinking about what happened.	
33	*Flashback:* White Mike's mother's funeral.	Whole chapter in *italics*
34	Chris in the "wrapping room" the existence of which underlines the wealth of the Upper East Side.	

Ch.	Contents	Comments
35	*Flashback:* White Mike's thoughts at the funeral. He thinks about leaving his mark on the world or being forgotten after death.	Literature: *Camus;* whole chapter in *italics*
36	Chris and Claude at the cocktail party. Generation gap underlined.	Music: Eminem, *Imagine* (John Lennon and Yoko Ono)
37	Jessica has done all her Twelve already.	Three-line chapter
38	White Mike sells drugs to Tobias. *Flashback:* Mike and Alice talking about first times.	Literature: *The Plague*
39	Claude and Tobias in Chinatown again. Claude leaves Tobias, although he originally wanted his company. Claude gets his Uzi.	
40	White Mike dreams about falling from a skyscraper.	
41	*Flashback:* Alice running into the cold ocean during Christmas break.	Literature: *A Christmas Carol* ("Ghost of Christmas Past")
	Part III – **Sunday, December 29**	
42	*Flashback:* Alice and White Mike. Alice speculates on why Mike does not drink.	Eight-line chapter; whole chapter in *italics*
43	Chris's boxing lesson: he is interrupted by Sara who wants to go into more detail about the party. Chris gives in and agrees to let Sara host the party at his house. Sara knows about Jessica's connection to "Twelve".	
44	Chris and Claude. Claude works on his Uzi. Chris wonders why he is so patient. Both take a shower in their bathrooms.	
45	Molly visits White Mike. She doesn't know he is a dealer and Mike acts as if he weren't. It is emphasized how well White Mike knows the "scene": "I am those parties."	
46	First part of Andrew's meeting with Sven: they play chess in a park.	
47	*Flashback:* White Mike meets a bum called "Captain".	Whole chapter in *italics*
48	Second part of Andrew's meeting with Sven. Sven lectures Andrew concerning his language and his future. Contrast between old man who has traveled the world and knows about hardship and youngster who doesn't really care about anything.	Literature: *The Old Man and the Sea; Caesar; Catullus*
49	White Mike tries to recover an ounce of marijuana from a hole at a construction site. Foreshadowing of disaster in the end (→ Mike encounters a rat down there which – according to Camus – is a symbol of death).	
50	Claude with a sword in front of a mirror.	
51	Captain freaks out and White Mike calls 911.	
	Part IV – **Monday, December 30**	
52	Andrew calls Sara who invites him to the party. She urges him to bring some weed; Andrew doesn't know where to get it from.	Music: *Sublime*
53	Timmy and Mark Rothko enter the scene. They offer some comic relief with their pseudo-gangster behaviour.	Art: *Mark Rothko: Untitled (Number Twelve)*

Ch.	Contents	Comments
54	White Mike on the phone with Warren. They make small talk until Mike gets upset for no apparent reason and decides to go to Coney Island.	Literature: *Dante*
55	Sean at home and on his way to hospital. Another example of a spoiled upper-class kid with no manners.	Film: *Taxi Driver*
56	White Mike on Coney Island walking around and pondering. He thinks about how he actually likes to go to church.	Literature: *Ragtime*
57	White Mike on his way to meet Timmy and Mark Rothko. He has a very self-confident moment walking down Fifth Avenue.	
58	"Fuckin' forty-fifth Street? What in the damn shiz fo a niz?"	Shortest chapter in the book
59	*Flashback:* White Mike on his way to the dermatologist's office walking down Fifth Avenue watching people. "I'll never be old."	
60	White Mike at FAO Schwarz.	
61	*Flashback:* Mark Rothko gets a fake ID.	
62	Jessica in her room with expensive stuffed animals imitating a talk show and fantasizing about a school massacre.	End of chapter = epigraph
63	Timmy and Mark Rothko try to buy some cigarettes. Again: comic relief.	
64	*Flashback:* White Mike at the dermatologist's office. He thinks about jobs and which job he will have one day.	Whole chapter in *italics*
65	Jessica has lunch with her mother who seems to sense trouble. But her only solution is to offer her daughter sessions at a psychiatrist's.	
66	White Mike sells drugs to Timmy and Mark Rothko who arrange a deal with Andrew.	
67	*Flashback*: White Mike watches skateboarders at the amphitheatre in Central Park.	Whole chapter in *italics*
68	Hunter in jail finally talking to his father after almost two days.	
69	Hunter's father thinks about a terrible accident in his youth in which one kid was killed. He could have prevented it but didn't and he was not held responsible. Reality was just shoved aside.	
70	*Flashback:* White Mike in ethics class making obscene comments about religion ("giving God a blow job").	Whole chapter in *italics*
71	White Mike and Andrew at the amphitheatre in Central Park. Andrew is very self-conscious which Mike realizes. Mike wants to make him think about life, almost lecturing him.	
72	*Flashback:* New Year's Eve the year before. White Mike/thinking about the gap between happiness and sadness so close together in New York.	
73	*Flashback*: White Mike spends some time with his father who doesn't know anything about Mike and has trouble keeping up with his own life.	Whole chapter in *italics*
74	Molly tries to find an outfit for the party. She seems totally unsure of herself and throws a tank top out of her window.	

Part V – New Year's Eve

Ch.	Contents	Comments
75	*Flashback:* White Mike accompanies Hunter during a bad drug trip around Manhattan.	Whole chapter in *italics*
76	Andrew's day leading up to the party. He is very self-conscious (parallel to Molly, cf. both in front of the mirror).	
77	Molly jumps rope to fight her nervousness.	
78	Chris buys condoms in case he has sex at his party. He is also very self-conscious.	
79	Chris throws away his porn magazines feeling as if it is a coming of age ritual.	
80	*Flashback:* White Mike observes a family living opposite his house with binoculars.	
81	Chris and Claude. Chris informs Claude about the party. Claude doesn't care and goes back into his candle-lit room to admire himself with his sword. His weapons make him feel better than drugs.	
82	White Mike buys some ornithological books. Timmy and Mark Rothko follow him. Mike lets them into his apartment and talks about the parrot he wants to get.	Music: *Snoop Doggy Dog* Comic relief
83	Hunter on the phone with his dad who is about to bail him out. Hunter admits he is scared for the first time.	
84	Timmy and Mark Rothko eat crackers in a grocery store and break a jar. They also want to go to the party.	
85	White Mike learns about Charlie's death and starts cleaning the apartment in a frenzy. Finally he goes out for a walk.	
86	Jessica prepares for the party, only thinking about Twelve. She's very self-confident.	
87	White Mike in church trying to get a clear head. He tries to think of Charlie.	
88	The party begins. Jessica is nervous about Lionel and "Twelve". Claude is uneasy in his room. Some girl calls White Mike's beeper from Jessica's phone.	Music: *Rolling Stones, D'Angelo, Weezer*
89	White Mike in a cab from the church to his apartment. In the end his beeper goes off → the girl from chapter 88.	Parallel editing like in a movie
90	Some people at the party talk about Hunter and whether he really might have killed Nana.	
91	Lionel arrives and meets Jessica who offers him sex for "Twelve" and starts to undress.	
92	The party gets into full swing. Scene in the kitchen where Andrew meets Molly. This could be a scene from any teenager party. Short *flashback:* Chris remembers how he lighted matches at the door of his parents' bedroom to scare his mother.	
93	White Mike walks towards Chris's house starting quite fast until he breaks into a run.	
94	White Mike enters the party and starts to freak out. He destroys the stereo and attacks Chris.	Music: *Bob Marley*

Ch.	Contents	Comments
95	Everybody goes to see what is happening with White Mike and Chris except Molly and Andrew who talk about parties, a subject they both don't know anything about. Outside the kitchen White Mike punches Chris.	
96	White Mike looks for Jessica. He searches the house and the crowd follows him. He doesn't hear Molly calling him.	
97	White Mike catches Lionel and Jessica in the act, and as Lionel pulls Charlie's gun Mike realizes that Lionel killed Charlie. Lionel shoots, which triggers Claude to enter the scene and shoot wildly with his Uzi leaving eight people dead. Coming out of the house he is shot by the police.	Denouement
Afterword		
98	White Mike reveals himself as the narrator of the book. He tells the reader that he lives and studies in Paris now, where he even smokes pot.	Whole chapter in *italics*

The author

Nick McDonell was born on February 18, 1984 in New York City. His parents, Joanie and Terry, were divorced so he grew up in two households in the Upper East Side of Manhattan. He attended Riverdale Country School, a prestigious private school in New York City.

Both his parents are in the writing and editing business. His mother Joanie is a novelist herself and his father Terry is the editor of *Sports Illustrated*, so he grew up in an environment of books and reading and has early memories of his parents reading him stories like *Huckleberry Finn*. As soon as he started reading himself he also began to write.

So it comes as no surprise that his first novel *Twelve* was published when McDonell was only 17, just after he graduated from high school in 2002. Yet some critics claim that it was not hard for him to get published, as his editor was also his godfather. Nevertheless, *Twelve* was praised by critics all over the world and the novel has been translated into 20 languages and published in 22 countries so far. He was inspired by the Columbine rampage in 1999 as well as by what he had experienced in 17 years of living in New York City, and it took him only nine weeks to actually write the novel.

From 2002–2007 he attended Harvard College, one of the most famous colleges in the world. In September 2005 his second novel, *The Third Brother,* was published, in which he tells the story of a Harvard student during an internship at an international magazine in Thailand. The second part of the novel deals with the events around 9/11/2001. His third novel, *An Expensive Education,* was published in August 2009 and is set partly in Harvard and partly in Somalia.

Besides his career as a novelist, McDonell is also active as a journalist and has written for *Harper's* and *Time,* for which he reported from distant places such as Sudan and Iraq.

Vorüberlegungen zum Einsatz des Romans im Unterricht

Im Jahr 2002 wurde Nick McDonells Roman *Twelve* in den USA veröffentlicht. Das Debüt des damals 17-jährigen Amerikaners wurde ein Sensationserfolg. Die Kritikerin Joan Didion schrieb: „Nick McDonell's TWELVE is an astonishing rush of a first novel, all heat and ice and inexorable narrative drive – the kind of novel you finish and immediately read again, just to see how it works. And it does work – a pleasure to read, a horror to contemplate, a real achievement." (www.groveatlantic.com)

Schülerinnen und Schüler sind davon fasziniert, dass *Twelve* von einem 17-Jährigen geschrieben wurde. Die Vorstellung, selbst ein Buch zu schreiben, liegt den meisten Jugendlichen in diesem Alter zwar fern, jedoch macht die Tatsache, dass dies einem Gleichaltrigen gelungen ist, neugierig auf den Inhalt. Die Protagonisten des Buches sind ebenfalls um die 17, was die Auseinandersetzung mit den Charakteren leicht macht. Die Schülerinnen und Schüler wollen die Handlungen der Romanfiguren verstehen und nachvollziehen. Sie erkennen, dass diese Charaktere Probleme damit haben, ihre Identität zu finden, in ihrer Umwelt zurechtzukommen. Die Tatsache, dass die Handlung im Milieu der superreichen Bewohner der Upper East Side von Manhattan spielt, schafft wiederum eine gewisse Distanz, welche die Reflexion und den kritischen Umgang mit den Verhaltensweisen der Jugendlichen im Roman erleichtert.
Nick McDonell schreibt in einem teils expliziten Jugendjargon, der die Schülerinnen und Schüler überrascht. Zugleich werden sie motiviert, *Twelve* zu lesen und mit dem Roman zu arbeiten. Ein weiterer motivierender Faktor ist die Musik. Künstler wie Nelly, Tupac, Ben Harper, Bob Marley und viele andere werden im Buch erwähnt und schaffen dort eine Atmosphäre, die von unseren Schülerinnen und Schülern verstanden und gefühlt wird. Das Buch hat einen regelrechten „Soundtrack", der den Unterricht begleiten und zuweilen bestimmen kann.
Auch die Montage des Buches, das zurzeit von Joel Schumacher verfilmt wird, passt zur Popmusik. Die teils sehr kurzen Kapitel sind wie in einem Film um die Hauptperson, den Drogendealer White Mike, arrangiert. Das Genre „Roman" kann so mit dem Genre „Film" verknüpft werden, das den Schülerinnen und Schülern heutzutage oft vertrauter und näher ist. Grundbegriffe der Filmanalyse können hier in einem anderen Zusammenhang eingeführt oder wiederholt werden.

Die Seiten- und Zeilenangaben dieses Unterrichtsmodells beziehen sich auf die annotierte Reclam-Ausgabe (ISBN 978-3-15-009127-2).

Klausuren

Voraussetzung für beide im Folgenden vorgeschlagenen Klausuren ist, dass die Schülerinnen und Schüler den Roman ganz gelesen haben. Das Niveau der Klausuren ist unterschiedlich; die erste Klausur wird für Klasse 10 empfohlen, die zweite für Klasse 11 aufwärts.

Ein großer Teil des **Klausurvorschlags 1** beruht auf der Reproduktion von Inhalten, die bei der Arbeit mit *Twelve* besprochen wurden. In der letzten Aufgabe wählen die Schülerinnen und Schüler zwischen zwei kreativen Schreibaufträgen.
Entweder schreiben sie Jessicas Geständnis bei einem Psychiater, oder sie verfassen einen Brief, in dem White Mike seinem Vater erklärt, wie es zur Katastrophe kam. Es ist auch denkbar, einige der hier gestellten Aufgaben als „warm-up" für die zweite, anspruchsvollere Klausur zu verwenden.

Klausurvorschlag 2 bezieht sich auf Kapitel 49 des Romans, das die Lerngruppe zunächst inhaltlich in den Roman einordnen muss. Die Schwierigkeit liegt hier darin, dass der Roman viele Handlungsstränge hat und nicht alle von ihnen zusammengefasst werden können.
Die Schülerinnen und Schüler müssen abwägen, welche Stränge unbedingt für eine kohärente Zusammenfassung notwendig sind.

Ein weiterer Schwerpunkt einer Klausur könnte beispielsweise das Verfassen einer Charakterisierung von White Mike sein (vgl. 7.3, S. 95), wenn diese nicht bereits Gegenstand des Unterrichts war und/oder die Musercharakterisierung verwendet wurde.

Nick McDonell: *Twelve*

Assignments

I. Comprehension questions

1. What is *comic relief* and how is it realized in Nick McDonell's *Twelve*?

2. What is a *flat character*? Give an example from *Twelve*.

3. What is a *round character*? Give an example from *Twelve*.

4. Explain the point of view taken in *Twelve* and its connection to the language that is used.

5. Sara Ludlow wants to be famous. Explain how she plans to accomplish this goal and how she overcomes the problems she faces.

6. What is the *butterfly effect*? Give two examples of how this notion applies to *Twelve*.

II. Text production

Choose **one** of the following assignments:

1. After the massacre Jessica is seeing a psychiatrist. She is so shocked by what happened that it makes her change for the good. Write her confession in which she explains why she acted the way she did.

or

2. Imagine White Mike writes a letter from Paris to his father in which he tries to explain what happened to Charlie and what happened at the party. Write this letter.

Erwartungshorizont zu Klausur 1

zu I. 1: Comic relief is something funny that appears in a plot that is mostly sad or depressing. In *Twelve* Timmy and Mark Rothko, two white kids, offer comic relief with their ridiculous imitation of black gangster rappers. They dress like them, walk like them and talk like them.

zu I. 2: A flat character is static and only built around a single quality. There is not much individual detail given. Examples in *Twelve*: Tobias, Lionel, Alice, Hunter, Nana, Timmy and Mark Rothko, Jessica.

zu I. 3: A round character is dynamic and develops in the course of the story and is complex in temperament and motivation (similar to a person in reality). Example in *Twelve*: White Mike.

zu I. 4: *Twelve* is written from the point of view of an omniscient third-person narrator. In each chapter he takes on the point of view of the character in the centre of interest.
By the same token, the language used depends on the character in focus. For example in chapters which focus on White Mike there is both slang and educated language (standard English).

zu I. 5: cf. 3.2 (S. 47), "I'm not a slut" – Sara's way of becoming famous.

zu I. 6: cf. **Copy 31** (S. 99)

zu II. 1: Offen für die Lösungen der Schülerinnen und Schüler; Jessica wird ihre Drogengeschichte erzählen und dabei sicherlich nicht ihre Mutter verschonen. Eventuell wird sie auch auf Sara Ludlows Rolle und die hedonistische Mentalität der Jugendlichen der Upper East Side eingehen.

zu II. 2: Offen für die Lösungen der Schülerinnen und Schüler. Eine zentrale Rolle muss jedoch der Tod von White Mikes Mutter spielen und die Einsamkeit, die er empfand, weil sein Vater mit sich selbst und seiner Arbeit beschäftigt war. Die Rolle der anderen Erwachsenen wird White Mike ebenfalls wichtig sein.

Text: Excerpt from: Nick McDonell, *Twelve* (chapter 49, pp. 118/119)

Assignments

1. Place the passage in the overall context of the novel.
2. Explain the concept of *foreshadowing* in the context of this passage.
3. Outline White Mike's emotional development from the time of the incident described in the passage to the end of the novel.

Erwartungshorizont zu Klausur 2

zu 1: Nach einer kurzen Einleitung wird die Handlung bis zur gegebenen Textstelle kurz zusammengefasst, die Textstelle eingeordnet und der Rest der Handlung umrissen:

White Mike, a drug dealer, is the main character in Nick McDonell's *Twelve* which was published in 2002. In the given scene he recovers a bag of marijuana which fell into a hole at a construction site.

It's shortly after Christmas and two days after a house party at Chris's place. His parents are not at home during Christmas break, like many other parents of the Upper East Side. At the party, a girl called Jessica tries out a new drug called "Twelve". The same day, another drug dealer is killed somewhere in Harlem.

The next day, another girl called Sara comes up with the plan to throw an even bigger party to make her famous. She talks Chris into having the party and starts spreading the news. All the characters in the novel know about the party and White Mike, of course, plays an important part, as he is supposed to deliver the drugs.

The given scene is set on a Sunday. Everything is quite calm and nobody has anything to do. Molly, a friend of White Mike's who actually doesn't know he's a drug dealer, has just come around for a visit, because she's not sure whether she wants to go to the party or not. Later, Mike goes to a drug deal alone. After the deal, a bag of drugs accidently falls into a hole at a construction site.

White Mike spends the Monday after the given scene mostly wandering aimlessly and dealing drugs. The other characters get more and more nervous before the big New Year's Eve party.

On the day of the party, New Year's Eve, White Mike learns that his cousin was killed, which finally makes him go to the big party where he freaks out, causing another dealer to shoot at him. The gunfire brings Claude, the host's brother, out of his room who shoots eight guests and is finally shot by the police.

zu 2: *Foreshadowing* is a narrative technique of implying or hinting at what is going to happen. In the given passage White Mike climbs down a ladder into a hole which he thinks is dry and well-lit. As he climbs down he realizes that the opposite is the case. It's dark and humid. While he searches for the bag of marijuana a rat scurries by. In an earlier chapter, White Mike thinks about Albert Camus' *The Plague* in which rats are depicted as symbols of death. So the darkness and a rat that crosses White Mike's path in the hole can be understood as a means of foreshadowing death.

zu 3: In the given passage, White Mike already feels slightly uncomfortable about being a drug dealer. In the remainder of the novel he becomes very confused and highly aggressive.

The only passages till the end in which White Mike is amused are the ones in which he encounters Timmy and Mark Rothko. They offer him – and the reader – comic relief. In all his other appearances he becomes more and more contemplative and, finally, aggressive. This starts when he hangs up on his friend Warren and leaves for Coney Island, where he wanders aimlessly and is scared by the presence of another dealer.

On New Year's Eve, the day of the party, Timmy and Mark Rothko follow him home, which makes him feel uneasy and angry. The real turning point, however, is when White Mike's father calls him to tell him that his cousin Charlie was shot in a drug deal. Charlie was like a brother to him and White Mike was already worried because he hadn't heard from Charlie in a while. After an initial outburst of screams and aggression, he cleans the apartment and goes to a church where he tries to calm down. For a short while he goes home again, but can't stand his father's presence. He starts walking to a house party where a girl called Jessica has called him several times to buy drugs. He seems to realize that the life he and all the other kids of the Upper East Side are leading is not the way he wants to live. As Charlie was also a drug dealer, he realizes that drug dealing is a dangerous business; perhaps he is also afraid of getting caught by the police.

His growing tension and aggression is shown as he walks faster and faster until he starts to run. Arriving at the party, he wants to meet Jessica, whom he knows to be slipping into a drug addiction. After hitting the party's host in the face, he finds Jessica in bed with another dealer, whom he identifies as Charlie's murderer. This is the highpoint of his aggression and, although held at gunpoint, he goes after the dealer who shoots and injures him. The gunfire attracts the attention of Claude. Claude is the host's brother, a former cocaine-addict and a weapon buff, who ends the party with a shooting rampage, leaving eight guests dead.

In conclusion, White Mike's mood develops from a slightly uneasy feeling into a state of extreme aggression.

Konzeption des Unterrichtsmodells

Ziel des vorliegenden Unterrichtsmodells ist die intensive Auseinandersetzung der Schülerinnen und Schüler mit dem Roman *Twelve* auf verschiedenen Ebenen: Neben Aspekten der Romananalyse gibt es auch kreative und handlungsorientierte Aufgabenstellungen zum Roman, seinen Figuren und seinen Themen. Die methodischen Anleitungen für die Arbeit mit *Twelve* werden durch Arbeitsblätter unterstützt.

Die Aufgabenstellungen bieten viele Sprechanlässe für die Schülerinnen und Schüler. Unterrichtsgesprächen sind oft vorbereitende Partner- oder Gruppenphasen vorgeschaltet. Dies erleichtert schwächeren Schülerinnen und Schülern die Teilnahme am Plenum und bietet stärkeren die Möglichkeit, Verantwortung für den Lernerfolg der Gruppe zu übernehmen.

Das Unterrichtsmodell sieht ein begleitendes Lesen des Romans vor, die *Components* sind analog zum Verlauf des Romans angeordnet. Lediglich *Component 4* kann auch zu einem späteren Zeitpunkt bearbeitet werden. Falls nicht ausreichend Zeit für die Bearbeitung aller Aktivitäten des Unterrichtsmodells zur Verfügung steht, können einzelne Teile weggelassen werden, ohne das Textverständnis zu beeinträchtigen. Diese sind im Folgenden als „optional" gekennzeichnet.

Component 1 beinhaltet *pre-reading activities*, die die Neugier der Schülerinnen und Schüler wecken sollen. Nick McDonell schrieb den Roman im Alter von 17 Jahren. Können sich die Schülerinnen und Schüler auch vorstellen, einen Roman zu schreiben? Außerdem soll durch die Aktivitäten eine Atmosphäre geschaffen werden, die Lust auf die Geschichte macht. Erst am Ende des *Components* werden die Textausgaben verteilt und die Schülerinnen und Schüler lernen White Mike kennen.

In **Component 2** stellen sich die Schülerinnen und Schüler gegenseitig weitere Romanfiguren vor. Im Umgang mit den Figuren werden Grundbegriffe der Charakterisierung eingeführt. Nach der Untersuchung der Erzählperspektive erhalten die Schülerinnen und Schüler abschließend Gelegenheit, über ihre Leseeindrücke zu sprechen.

Component 3 hat zwei Schwerpunkte: Zum einen wird der Fortgang der Handlung genau unter die Lupe genommen, um klarzustellen, dass White Mike die Figur ist, die im Mittelpunkt des Geschehens steht. Zum anderen wird die Drogenproblematik thematisiert. In einer Art Rollenspiel nimmt die Lerngruppe an einem Kongress für Mitarbeiter der Drogenhilfe teil.

Zwei Gründe, warum der Roman bei Jugendlichen im Allgemeinen gut ankommt, sind seine Sprache und die Musik, die die Handlung begleitet. Beides wird in **Component 4** behandelt. Wenn die Lerngruppe aber lieber weiterlesen möchte, kann der *Component* auch später bearbeitet werden. Am Ende finden sich Vokabellisten für jeden Teil des Romans, die teils Wörter aus dem Roman und teils ergänzendes Vokabular enthalten. Optional: „The songs in part I and II" (4.1, S. 54).

Teil 3 ist der kürzeste und zugleich „langsamste" im Roman. Die Szenenwechsel erfolgen nicht so schnell wie in den anderen Teilen. **Component 5** trägt dem Rechnung, indem er den langsameren Lebensrhythmus an Sonntagen thematisiert. Darüber hinaus geht es um die Leidenschaftslosigkeit der Jugendlichen und um erste Zweifel, die in White Mike aufkommen. Die Ratten aus Albert Camus' „Die Pest" dienen als Aufhänger, um den Begriff des *foreshadowing* einzuführen. Optional: „What's your passion?" (5.2, S. 72).

Component 6 gibt Anleitungen zur Auseinandersetzung mit komplexen Beziehungen auf verschiedenen Ebenen. Jessica, Andrew und White Mike werden mit ihren Eltern in eine Familientherapie geschickt, um ihre gestörten Beziehungen zu verbessern. Außerdem erstellen die Schülerinnen und Schüler zur Veranschaulichung des komplexen Beziehungsgeflechts eine grafische Figurenkonstellation des Romans, in dessen Zentrum White Mike steht. Über ihn lassen sich fast alle Figuren miteinander in Verbindung bringen. Optional: „White Mike – the center of the novel" (6.2, S. 84).

Component 7 legt schließlich einen Schwerpunkt auf *post-reading activities*. White Mikes Entwicklung in Teil 5 wird genau beleuchtet, um seinen Anteil am Massaker zu verdeutlichen. Weitere Aktivitäten sind die Charakterisierung White Mikes, der Entwurf von Filmszenen aus Teil 5 sowie die Untersuchung des Romans vor dem Hintergrund des *butterfly effect*, der schon im ersten Kapitel erwähnt wird. Mit einer Aufzählung weiterer Ideen für *post-reading activities* endet das Unterrichtsmodell. Optional: „It's like a movie" (7.2, S. 91) und „The butterfly effect and *Twelve*" (7.4, S. 98).

Component 1

Sparking curiosity

Pre-reading activities sind essenziell für die Lesemotivation und damit auch für das spätere Textverständnis der Schülerinnen und Schüler; mit ihnen werden die emotionalen Weichen für die gesamte Lesephase gestellt. Deshalb sollte relativ viel Zeit dafür aufgewendet werden, die Lektüre des Romans vorzubereiten.

Der erste *Component* verfolgt dieses Ziel in drei Schritten. Zuerst wird die Tatsache thematisiert, dass der Autor erst 17 war, als er den Roman schrieb. Den meisten Schülerinnen und Schülern liegt die Vorstellung fern, selbst zu schreiben, dennoch wird hier Interesse für das Buch geweckt. Anschließend soll Atmosphäre geschaffen und die Neugierde der Schülerinnen und Schüler geweckt werden. Schließlich erfolgt das Eintauchen in den Plot: Die ersten Seiten werden gelesen, um den Dreh- und Angelpunkt des Romans, White Mike, kennenzulernen. Außerdem wird das Milieu vorgestellt, in dem der Roman spielt.

1.1 Writing a novel at 17!?

Im ersten Schritt soll auf die Tatsache hingewiesen werden, dass der Autor erst 17 Jahre alt war, als er den Roman schrieb, also etwa im Alter der Schülerinnen und Schüler. Hierzu stellt die Lehrerkraft Nick McDonell mit einer Bildfolie und einem kurzen Vortrag vor. Als Grundlage hierfür können die Informationen über den Autor (S. 14) verwendet werden.

Paarweise machen sich die Schülerinnen und Schüler im Anschluss daran Gedanken über mögliche Themen und Geschichten eines von ihnen zu verfassenden Romans, die stichwortartig festgehalten werden.

> You are writing a novel. What is it about?
> Write down keywords about the characters, the plot, and the setting (time and place).

Nun wird die Mitte des Klassenzimmers freigeräumt, damit die Ideen ausgetauscht werden können. Dazu muss jede Schülerin/jeder Schüler auf diesem „Forum" mit möglichst vielen Mitschülern und Mitschülerinnen über die jeweiligen Ideen sprechen und diskutieren.

> Where are differences between the story ideas?
> Where are similarities?
> Which of the other groups' ideas do you like/dislike?

1.2 Creating atmosphere

Im zweiten Schritt wird auf das Epigraf des Buches eingegangen, das möglicherweise Hinweise auf die Geschichte gibt, die Nick McDonell sich ausgedacht hat. Die Schülerinnen und Schüler versammeln sich in der immer noch freien Mitte des Raumes. Die auf Folie kopierte Einstiegsseite „Getting started" (S. 3) sollte jetzt aufgelegt werden. Zusätzlich kann feierliche

Musik gespielt werden (z. B. Johann Pachelbels *Kanon in D*). Die Schülerinnen und Schüler stehen, die Lehrkraft liest den Text laut vor.

Jetzt schreiben die Schülerinnen und Schüler stichwortartig ihre Gedanken darüber auf, unter welchen Umständen es zu den Todesfällen gekommen sein könnte, wer zu Tode gekommen und wer dafür verantwortlich sein könnte.

Anschließend bekommen die Schülerinnen und Schüler die Möglichkeit, ihre Ideen an die Tafel zu schreiben; es sollten mehrere Kreiden zur Verfügung stehen, damit kein „Stau" an der Tafel entsteht. Die Tafel kann während der Arbeitsphase vorstrukturiert werden, um das anschließende Gespräch zu erleichtern. Das Tafelbild könnte so aussehen:

Twelve – who might die and why?

Who?	How?	Why?	By whom?
• high school students • college students	• gunman • accident • taking of hostages • gang fights	• frustration • anger • boredom • desperation • rivalry	• students gone crazy • outsiders • gang members

> Who would like to comment on these speculations?
> Is there anything that sounds very likely/unlikely to you?

Zwar findet das Massaker erst am Ende des Romans statt und ist kein zentrales Thema der eigentlichen Geschichte; es kann aber Neugierde und Interesse für das Buch schaffen. Vorbereitend für das Lesen des ersten Kapitels bietet sich eine arbeitsteilige Internetrecherche als Hausaufgabe an: Ein Teil der Klasse/des Kurses beschäftigt sich hierzu mit Besonderheiten der *Upper East Side* in Manhattan, der andere Teil mit den Privatcolleges, die im Text erwähnt werden. Hierzu erhält jede Schülerin/jeder Schüler das Arbeitsblatt *Copy 1*. Die Besprechung der Hausaufgabe in der nächsten Sitzung erfolgt zunächst in Partnerarbeit, indem jeweils ein Partner dem anderen seine Ergebnisse vorstellt.

Lösungsmöglichkeiten zu *Copy 1*:

> **Partner A:**
> **Geography**: The Upper East Side is situated in Manhattan, one of the five boroughs of NYC, between Central Park and East River.
> **Real estate**: Very expensive apartments (150 m² for more than $ 1 million), often the buildings have full-time doormen.
> **Inhabitants**: The Upper East Side is a place inhabited by very rich people. Celebrities such as Beyoncé Knowles and Bruce Willis have apartments there.
>
> **Partner B:**
> **Hotchkiss**: Prestigious private senior high school in Connecticut. Claims that most graduates attend selective colleges.
> **Andover**: Private school (elementary through high school) in Michigan; tuition fee for a high school year is more than $ 11,000.
> **Deerfield**: Private high school in Massachusetts, annual tuition: more than $ 40,000.

Partner A: The Upper East Side in Manhattan

Log on to the Internet and find out about the Upper East Side, a part of Manhattan in New York City. Write down what you find out about the categories below:

Geography (Where exactly is the Upper East Side?)	
Real estate (What are the apartments like there?)	
Inhabitants (Who lives there?)	

Partner B: Private boarding schools in the USA

Log on to the Internet and find out about the colleges mentioned below. Write down what you find special about each school.

Hotchkiss http://www.hotchkiss.org	
Andover http://www.andover.edu	
Deerfield http://www.deerfield.edu	

1.3 Getting to know White Mike

Nach der Besprechung der Hausaufgabe (*Copy 1*, S. 26) kann jetzt die Textausgabe ausgegeben werden. Die Schülerinnen und Schüler sollen sich zunächst mit dem Buch vertraut machen, es anfassen, anschauen, durchblättern, vielleicht sogar an den Seiten riechen! Die meisten Schülerinnen und Schüler bemerken in dieser Phase auch das Epigraf, das sie aus der letzten Stunde schon kennen; sie sind also schon etwas mit dem Buch vertraut. Die Überschrift von *Part I* „Friday, December 27" bietet die Möglichkeit, weiter Atmosphäre zu schaffen. Mögliche Impulse hierfür sind:

> 1. What comes to your mind when you read that date?
> 2. What did you do after Christmas last year?
> 3. What makes the time between Christmas and New Year's Eve special?

Jetzt lernen die Schülerinnen und Schüler White Mike kennen. Hierzu lesen sie etwas mehr als die erste Seite in Einzelarbeit.

> Now let's see what White Mike does on this day.
> Read up to p. 6, l. 5 silently to yourselves.
> Come up with an adjective that describes what you have just read. Write the word down on a slip of paper.

Die Schülerinnen und Schüler tauschen nun ihr Stück Papier jeweils mit einer/einem anderen. Jeder vergleicht das Adjektiv, das er bekommen hat, mit dem eigenen. Bevor die Paare über ihre Leseerfahrungen sprechen, überlegt sich jeder eine Frage, die er dem anderen gerne stellen möchte. Nach einem kurzen Gespräch über diese Fragen und die erste Seite des Romans überlegen sich die Partner gemeinsam, was sie White Mike gerne fragen würden. Diese Frage hält jede Schülerin/jeder Schüler schriftlich fest, um am Ende des Romans zu versuchen, sie zu beantworten. Da es sich hier um subjektive Eindrücke handelt, die den Schülerinnen und Schülern helfen sollen, in den Roman zu finden, werden die Adjektive und Fragen nicht im Plenum besprochen.
Jetzt lesen die Schülerinnen und Schüler weiter, um sich auf die Informationen zu konzentrieren, die der Leser auf den ersten zweieinhalb Seiten bekommt. Das Tafelbild kann während des Lesens von der Lehrkraft vorstrukturiert werden.

> Read up to p. 7, l. 6.
> 1. What do we learn about the setting and the characters of the story?
> 2. What is the function of the first two and a half pages of the novel?

Ein Tafelbild zur Ergebnissicherung könnte so aussehen:

> **The introductory pages**
>
> On pp. 5–7 we learn about
> - the main character White Mike and his ambivalence
> - the setting
>   a) time: Friday, December 27
>   b) place: Upper East Side, Manhattan
> - the people living there:
>   a) rich kids on holiday from private boarding schools
>   b) many homeless people on the streets
> - the weather: one of the coldest winters in years with lots of snow
>
> → **The introductory pages serve as an exposition and set the stage for the upcoming novel!**

Read the rest of chapter 1.

1. Start filling out the mind map about White Mike (*Copy 2*); don't forget to indicate where you found the information (page and line).

2. Read the info about characterization (*Copy 3*) and write down one fact about White Mike you have learned by means of showing technique and one by means of telling technique.

Keep adding facts to the mind map while you read the novel in order to record White Mike's development.

Die Mindmap über White Mike ist eine Aufgabe, die über die gesamte Lektüre hinweg erledigt werden muss. Die Schülerinnen und Schüler sollten sie deshalb immer in den Unterricht mitbringen, damit ggf. daran weitergearbeitet oder ein Abgleich mit den Versionen anderer stattfinden kann.

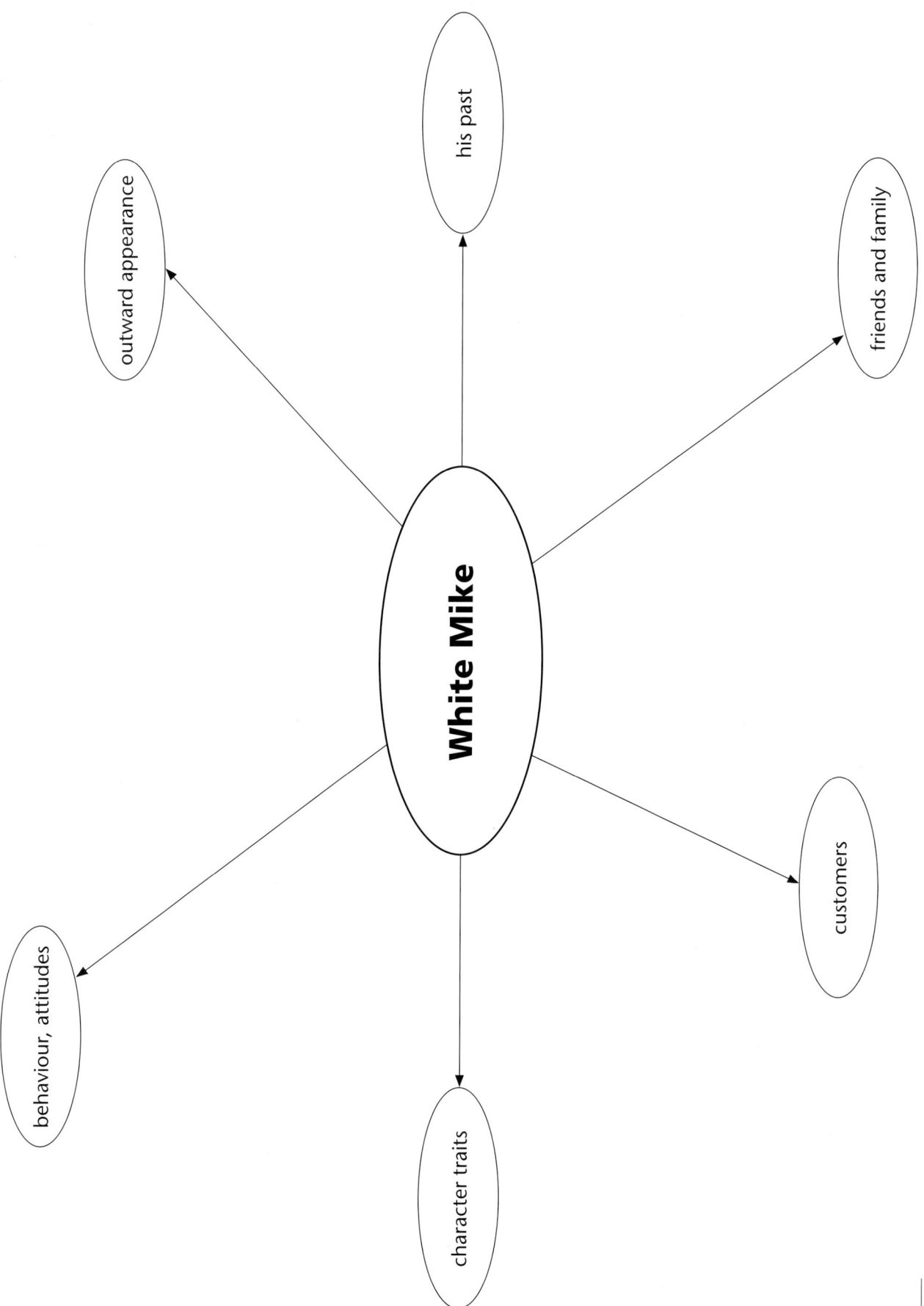

Talking about characters – Some important facts

> Definition: A character is a person in a dramatic or narrative work.
> A character may remain stable or may undergo a change/development.

Flat and round characters

flat = static, two-dimensional
- built around a single idea or quality
- presented without much individual detail

round = dynamic, three-dimensional
- complex in temperament and motivation (similar to a person in reality)
- develops over the course of the story

Types of characterization:
Showing technique   Telling technique

= indirect characterization
- we learn about the character from his appearance, actions, language, interaction, etc.
- the reader must "find out" the character traits
- example: a character tells a joke

= direct characterization
- the author tells the reader directly and explicitly about the figure's character traits
- often done by means of a narrator
- example: "The character was a very funny guy."

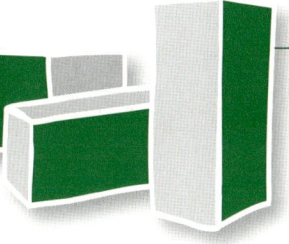

Component 2
Part I (pp. 5–48) – Getting to know the characters – and the book

Part I stellt die *Exposition* des Romans dar. Hier ist es wichtig, sich Zeit zu nehmen, um zentrale Figuren des Romans kennenzulernen. Außerdem wird die Struktur des gesamten Romans mit seinen kurzen Kapiteln und Sprüngen von Figur zu Figur deutlich. Romananalytisch sind die *Erzählperspektive* sowie die kursiv gedruckten *Flashbacks* interessant. Der *omniscient narrator* wechselt ständig die Perspektive und erzählt immer aus der Sicht der Figur, die im Mittelpunkt des jeweiligen Kapitels steht. Im ersten Teil dieses *Components* lernen die Schülerinnen und Schüler arbeitsteilig Figuren näher kennen, um sie dann in der Klasse vorzustellen. Als Hausaufgabe lesen sie dann *Part I* ganz, begleitet von einem Arbeitsblatt, das ihnen das Verständnis erleichtert. Hier werden auch die kurzen Kapitel thematisiert. Danach wird die Erzählperspektive beleuchtet und analysiert. Bevor den Schülerinnen und Schülern die Gelegenheit gegeben wird, über ihre ersten Leseeindrücke zu sprechen, beschäftigen sie sich immer wieder mit der Hauptperson, White Mike.

2.1 Who else is hanging around the Upper East Side?

Twelve lebt von den vielen verschiedenen Charakteren, die sich um White Mike tummeln. Umso wichtiger ist es für die Schülerinnen und Schüler, jeden Einzelnen auch zu kennen, um den Sprüngen von Figur zu Figur in den jeweiligen Kapiteln, folgen zu können. Zuerst sollen die Schülerinnen und Schüler Vermutungen anstellen, wen sie im Folgenden kennenlernen werden.

> **What other characters beside White Mike might be part of the novel? What might they be up to during their holidays?**

Die Hinweise aus *chapter 1* (S. 6, Z. 7 ff.) legen die Vermutung nahe, dass es sich vornehmlich um reiche Jugendliche handelt, die auf Geldausgeben, Partys und Drogen aus sind.

Die Schülerinnen und Schüler sollen sich jetzt vorstellen, an einem Austauschprogramm in New York teilgenommen zu haben. Dort haben sie eine der Figuren aus *Twelve* kennengelernt und erzählen nach der Rückkehr von dieser Figur. Die Arbeitsschritte der folgenden Einzel- und Gruppenarbeit (*Copies 5* und *6*) sind auf *Copy 4* zusammengefasst, die während der gesamten Arbeitsphase als Folie aufgelegt werden kann. So haben die Schülerinnen und Schüler immer einen Überblick über die Arbeit und die verbleibende Zeit, die mit Folienstift von der Lehrkraft eingetragen werden kann.
Es gilt, sechs Figuren des Romans zu untersuchen, deshalb muss jedem Schüler eine der Figuren zugeordnet werden. Zunächst lesen sie die zugeordneten Kapitel, um erste Notizen in *Copy 5* zu machen. Die Lehrkraft kann Fragen einzelner Schüler/innen beantworten und als Berater im Klassenraum fungieren. Der Leistungsstand der Klasse und der vorhandene Zeitrahmen (evtl. Doppelstunde) geben vor, wie lange die Einzelarbeit dauern und wie vollständig das Arbeitsblatt ausgefüllt werden soll. Zur Bearbeitung der Adjektive, welche

Introducing some characters in *Twelve*

1. Read the chapters that deal with the character you are assigned by your teacher:
   - Hunter: ch. 2, 3, and 5
   - Nana: ch. 2 and 6
   - Sara: ch. 7 and 11
   - Chris: ch. 9 and 14
   - Jessica: ch. 9 (only last paragraph) and 10
   - Claude: ch. 12

   Info: there's a party at Chris's house!

2. Now start filling out the worksheet "Some kid I met in New York."

3. At _____ you must form a group with the other students who are working on your character.

4. In your groups, compare what you have found out about your character and prepare a transparency to help you introduce your character in class.

5. Be ready to introduce your character at _____ .

6. While the characters are introduced, take notes so that you have all the necessary information in your exercise books!

Some kid I met in New York

Imagine that you were part of an exchange program in New York and you met the character you've just read about. Back home you are asked to introduce the character!

"In New York I met a kid named
_____ ."

Now, underline *two* adjectives from the box below or use others you know that best describe the character you are supposed to introduce.

aggressive – ambitious – arrogant – beautiful – bold – boring – bossy – calculating – calm – careless – clumsy – courageous – crazy – cruel – disciplined – educated – entertaining – evil – friendly – funny – honest – hostile – humorous – impulsive – insecure – intelligent – irresponsible – kind – lazy – likeable – lonely – mature – mean – modest – moody – naïve – nasty – open-minded – optimistic – outgoing – pessimistic – polite – quiet – reliable – respectful – rich – rude – self-confident – self-conscious – selfish – sensible – sensitive – serious – shallow – shy – sincere – sociable – sportive – talkative – tough – vain – violent – weird

Why did you choose these adjectives? Give examples from the text.

_____

_____

_____

_____

Try to find out about your character's *age*. Is it given by telling technique or showing technique? Write down where in the text you found the information.

_____

_____

What does he or she look like? Collect information from the text!

die Figur beschreiben sollen, bietet es sich ggf. in Klasse 10 an, Wörterbücher zur Verfügung zu stellen.

Eine kurze Beschreibung des Aussehens rundet diese Kurzcharakterisierung ab. Während der gesamten Aufgabe ist es wichtig, dass die Schülerinnen und Schüler ihre Antworten am Text belegen. Hier bietet sich ein Hinweis auf das richtige Zitieren und Verweisen an, also Anführungszeichen bei Zitaten, die Verwendung von *cf.* (= siehe) bei Verweisen, *p./pp. (= page/pages), l./ll. (= line/lines), f./ff. (= following line or page/following lines or pages)*.

Am Ende der vorgegebenen Zeit sollen sich jeweils alle Schülerinnen und Schüler, die dieselbe Figur bearbeitet haben, in Gruppen zusammenfinden, um ihre Ergebnisse zu vergleichen. Ein wichtiger Schritt dieser Phase ist, dass man sich in der Gruppe auf zwei beschreibende Adjektive einigt. Wer gute Gründe für die Wahl der Adjektive in der Einzelarbeit gefunden hat, kann seinen Standpunkt jetzt besser vertreten! Um die Figur im letzten Schritt strukturiert vorstellen zu können, erhält jede Gruppe eine Folie von **Copy 6** und Folienstifte. In den Bilderrahmen können die Gruppen ein Bild der Figur malen. Daneben sollten sie aber auf jeden Fall die verbale Beschreibung notieren. Die Lehrkraft kann den Kurs entweder anhalten mitzuschreiben oder die in den Gruppen erstellten Folien für alle kopieren. Selbstverständlich bietet diese Phase auch die Möglichkeit, den Präsentationsstil der Gruppen zu besprechen und zu verbessern. Als mögliche Kriterien eignen sich *Körpersprache* und *freies Sprechen*. Diesbezügliche Beobachtungsaufgaben können die Aufmerksamkeit in der Klasse erhöhen und zusätzlicher Ansporn für die Präsentierenden sein.

Folgende Lösungsmöglichkeiten ergeben sich für die einzelnen Figuren (*Copies 4, 5, 6*):

Hunter: He is likeable (p. 12, l. 10), friendly, polite (p. 12: he apologizes …), educated (p. 12, ll. 26 ff.: knowledge about Henry Clay), rich (pp. 19 ff.: description of his parents' apartment), sensitive (p. 21 f.: problematic father-son relationship).
As he is about to enter college, he is probably 18 years old (showing technique).
Hunter is 6 feet tall (ca. 1,80 m), "pretty beef," "stack of muscle and sinew" (p. 12, ll. 10 ff.).

Nana: He is fast and strong/athletic (p. 11, l. 7 f.), moody and selfish (p. 11, ll. 15 ff.: walks off and leaves his team), aggressive (pp. 12–15: fights Hunter), poor (p. 22: lives in the projects). Nothing is indicated about his age.
Nana's skin is "the color of coal" (p. 11, l. 8); he wears a white tank top (ibid.); he wears Jordans and a do-rag like all the other black kids at the Rec (p. 10, l. 10 f.).

Sara: She is "hot" (p. 25, l. 6), rich (p. 25, ll. 1 ff.: expensive designer stuff), "great-looking" (p. 25, l. 18), vain (p. 26, l. 4: looks into mirror while talking to friends), arrogant (p. 36, ll. 13 f.: does not show interest in Chris's story), calculating (p. 36, ll. 16 f.: "He might be useful").
Sara seems to be in senior high school and hopes to meet kids her age at Chris's house (p. 26, l. 6) → 17–18 years old.
Sara has "long legs, large breasts, blond hair, blue eyes, high cheekbones" (p. 25, ll. 16 f.).

Chris: He is naïve (p. 29, ll. 17 f.: thinks that Sara is really interested in him), self-conscious (pp. 28, 29: description of his awkward attempt to have sex; p. 29, l. 11: "lost his confidence"), rich (pp. 29, 30: description

The kid we met

Name: _____

He/she is _____ , because _____
_____
_____

He/she is _____ , because _____
_____
_____

Age: _____

How we found out about his/her age: _____
_____

What he/she looks like: _____
_____
_____

his/her picture!!

of his parents' house), awkward (p. 36, ll. 12f.: tells Sara a story about his brother's sex life).
Chris is 17½ years old (p. 28, l. 18).
He has dark blond hair, blue eyes, is quite good-looking but has acne (p. 28, ll. 19f.).

Jessica: She is vain (p. 32, l. 4: had a nose job), self-confident (p. 33, l. 4: talking about her body), intelligent (p. 34, ll. 3ff.: very good student, excellent college next year), careless (p. 33, ll. 12ff.: does cocaine and "Twelve", although she doesn't really know what "Twelve" is at first), athletic (p. 32, l. 16).
Jessica is a high school senior (p. 34, ll. 4f.: wants to go to college next year).
She is pretty, has creamy skin, long brown hair, big brown eyes, nice breasts, she is neither fat nor skinny, healthy-looking, has strong thighs, fine eyebrows (pp. 32, 33).

Claude: He is rich (p. 37: lots of cash, credit cards, etc.), either lazy or stupid (p. 38, ll. 5f.: fifth year of high school), aggressive (pp. 38, 39: story of him and the snake), offensive (p. 39: "Slantyville", p. 42: "tenk veddy much …"), strange, weird (pp. 38, 39: snake, p. 43: weapon shrine).
Claude is taking a fifth year of high school (p. 38, ll. 5f.), so he is older than eighteen.
He is six feet two inches tall (ca. 1,88 m), has fair and perfect skin, with a handsome, strong, angular face (p. 38, ll. 1ff.).

Die Bestimmung des Alters hängt – bis auf das Alter von Chris, das auf S. 28, Z. 18 explizit erwähnt ist, – davon ab, wie gut die Schülerinnen und Schüler mit dem amerikanischen Schulsystem vertraut sind, da meist nur indiziert wird, ob die Figuren noch die High School besuchen (wie Jessica, Sara und Claude, der allerdings ein fünftes Jahr dranhängen muss), oder ob sie bereits aufs College gehen (Hunter). Deshalb sollen sich die Schülerinnen und Schüler zu Hause über das amerikanische Schulsystem informieren und so das Alter „ihrer" Figur bestimmen.

Check the Internet for information about the American school system. Find out how old students are when they attend high school and college in order to guess "your" character's age.

Zur Besprechung in der nächsten Stunde kann *Copy 7* herangezogen werden.

The American school system

The following graph shows the classic American educational career. Compulsory schooling usually ends at the age of 16, but most teenagers graduate from high school at the age of 18. High school, as a part of public education, is free, while college and university charge tuition fees.

Age at the beginning of the schoolyear	School	Grade
22	University (Graduate school)	Graduate Students
21	College/ University (Undergraduate studies)	Seniors
20		Juniors
19		Sophomores
18		Freshmen
17	Senior High School	12th Seniors
16		11th Juniors
15		10th Sophomores
14		9th Freshmen
13	Middle School	8th
12		7th
11	Elementary School	6th
10		5th
9		4th
8		3rd
7		2nd
6		1st

2.2 A look back at part I

Part I wird auch in der nächsten Stunde noch Thema bleiben, weshalb er von den Schülerinnen und Schülern als weitere Hausaufgabe gelesen wird, noch haben sie ja nur Teile davon selbst gelesen. Das Arbeitsblatt „Looking back at part I" (*Copy 8* und *Copy 8a*) hilft dabei, genau zu lesen und nochmals auf die äußere Struktur des Romans aufmerksam zu machen. Die Straßenkarte (*Copy 9*) wird mit ausgeteilt, damit die Schülerinnen und Schüler die letzte Aufgabe des Arbeitsblattes ausfüllen können. Außerdem können sie die Karte immer wieder zur Hand nehmen, um nach Straßen und Orten zu suchen, die im Roman vorkommen.

For homework, do the worksheet "Looking back at part I" (*Copy 8*).
Keep adding facts to White Mike's mind map!

Nach dem kurzen Exkurs zum amerikanischen Schulsystem (s. 2.1, S. 37) am Stundenanfang ist es vor der Besprechung der zweiten Hausaufgabe sinnvoll, kurz mit den Schülerinnen und Schülern über ihre Leseerfahrungen zu sprechen.

Was it hard or easy to understand the text?
How did you like reading part I? Was it interesting or boring?
How long did it take to do the reading?

Sofern es der Zeitrahmen zulässt, sollte das Arbeitsblatt *Copy 8* vor der Besprechung im Plenum in Gruppenarbeit verglichen werden, um jeder Schülerin/jedem Schüler Sprechanlässe zu bieten. Außerdem können sich so auch schwächere Schüler leichter im Plenum einbringen, da zum einen eine erste Hemmschwelle schon überschritten ist und zum anderen Lösungen von stärkeren Schülern bekannt sind.

Looking back at part I

Read all the chapters in part I and do the tasks below.

1. How many chapters does part I have? _____

2. Why do you think there are so many chapters?
   _____
   _____
   _____

3. In how many chapters does White Mike appear? _____

4. Reread those chapters in order to continue the mind map on White Mike!

5. Some parts of the novel are printed in *italics*. How are those parts different from the parts in normal print?
   _____
   _____
   _____

6. There are three songs mentioned in part I. What are they called and who are the singers?

Name of song	Singer

7. Do you know any of these songs? Which one(s)? Do you know what genre of music the songs belong to or what the lyrics are about?
   _____
   _____
   _____

8. Answer the multiple choice questions on the characters below.

White Mike
- ☐ quit smoking
- ☐ has never smoked
- ☐ sells drugs
- ☐ all of the above
- ☐ none of the above

Chris
- ☐ is a womanizer
- ☐ has a perfect body
- ☐ doesn't smoke marijuana
- ☐ all of the above
- ☐ none of the above

Claude
- ☐ was at rehab
- ☐ loves weapons
- ☐ buys a skinned rabbit
- ☐ all of the above
- ☐ none of the above

Jessica
- ☐ doesn't do any sport
- ☐ had her nose done
- ☐ takes "Twelve"
- ☐ all of the above
- ☐ none of the above

9. Take the map your teacher gave you *(Copy 9)* to find and circle at least three places that are mentioned in the novel.

Looking back at part I (solutions)

Read all the chapters in part I and do the tasks below.

1. How many chapters does part I have? _____ 15 _____

2. Why do you think there are so many chapters?
There are many characters introduced in the novel. Each time the text changes to another character, a new chapter is started. So the chapters jump from character to character.

3. In how many chapters does White Mike appear? _____ 8 _____

4. Reread those chapters in order to continue the mind map on White Mike!

5. Some parts of the novel are printed in *italics*. How are those parts different from the parts in normal print?
In these parts the reader learns something about White Mike's past and his character. The tense changes from (simple) present to (simple) past.

6. There are three songs mentioned in part I. What are they called and who are the singers?

Name of song	Singer
Fire and rain	James Taylor
Ride wit me (must be the money)	Nelly
Burn one down	Ben Harper

7. Do you know any of these songs? Which one(s)? Do you know what genre of music the songs belong to or what the lyrics are about?
Taylor's song is a seventies ballad about a friend who has just died and how he thought he would meet her again. Nelly's rap song is about having a good time being a rich star with parties, drugs and women. Harper's acoustic guitar song is about how it's his own business whether he smokes marijuana or not.

8. Answer the multiple choice questions on the characters below.

White Mike
☐ quit smoking
☒ has never smoked
☒ sells drugs
☐ all of the above
☐ none of the above

Chris
☐ is a womanizer
☐ has a perfect body
☐ doesn't smoke marijuana
☐ all of the above
☒ none of the above

Claude
☐ was at rehab
☐ loves weapons
☐ buys a skinned rabbit
☒ all of the above
☐ none of the above

Jessica
☐ doesn't do any sport
☒ had her nose done
☒ takes "Twelve"
☐ all of the above
☐ none of the above

Streetmap of the Upper East Side

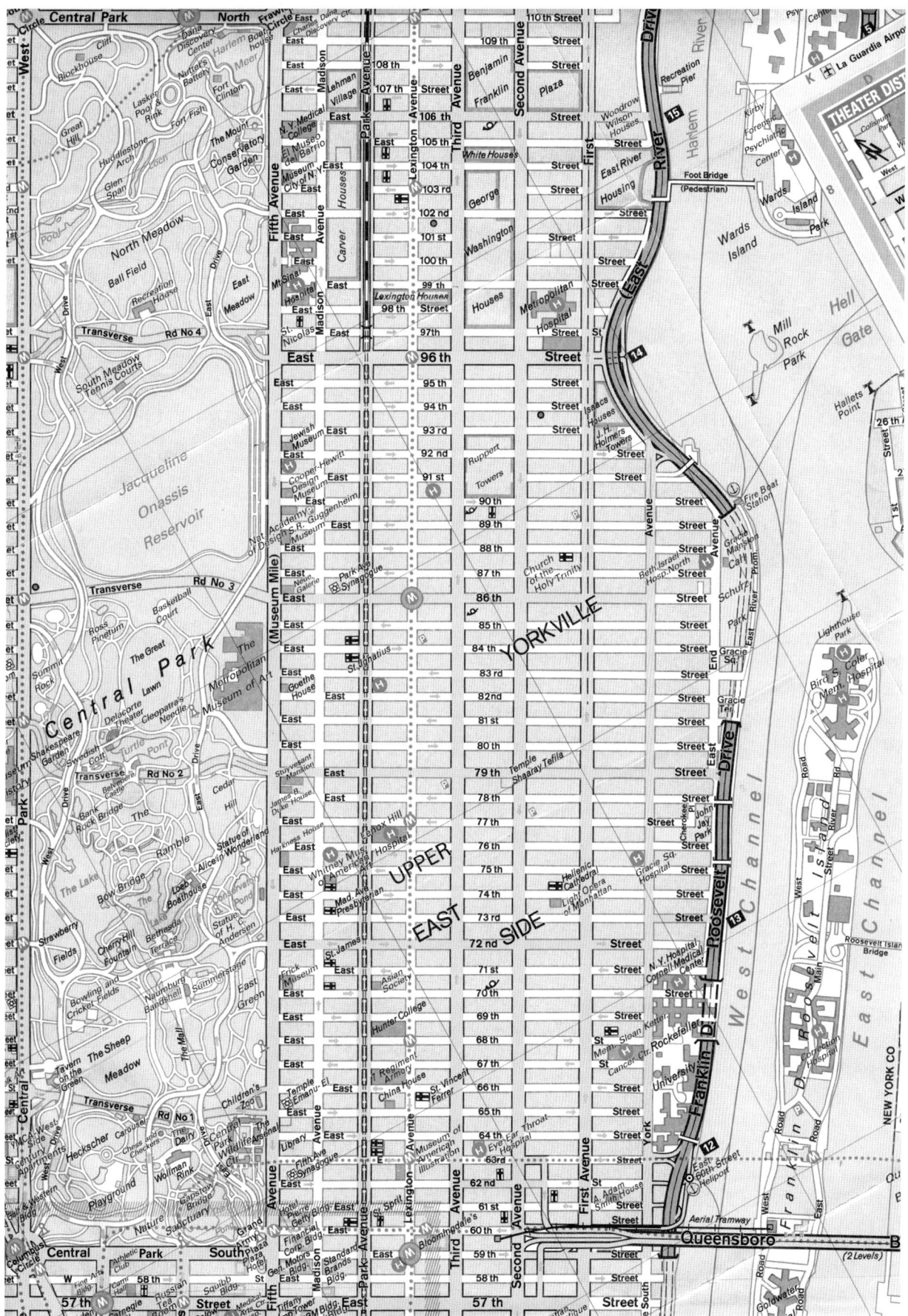

2.3 The point of view

Twelve wird von einem *allwissenden Erzähler* erzählt, der jedoch nicht durchgehend die gleiche Perspektive innehat, sondern diese in jedem Kapitel wechselt und aus der Sicht der unterschiedlichen Protagonisten schreibt, wodurch der Leser einen Einblick in ihre Gefühlswelt und ihr Handeln erhält. Einen besonderen Status hat jedoch White Mike, da er durch die kursiv gedruckten *Flashbacks* noch viel mehr Hintergrund bekommt als die anderen Figuren. Diese Fakten sollen im Unterrichtsgespräch herausgearbeitet werden, das durch folgende Leitfragen strukturiert werden kann:

1. What's the point of view of the narrator in *Twelve*?
2. Does the narrator have a limited point of view or does he know everything?
3. In what way is White Mike a special character with regard to point of view?

Ein Tafelbild zur Ergebnissicherung könnte so aussehen:

The point of view in *Twelve*

1. The narrator of the novel is an omniscient third-person narrator.
2. In each chapter the narrator takes on the perspective of the character that is the centre of interest.
   → But not all the characters are described in the same amount of detail. There is one protagonist whom we learn a lot more about!

3. White Mike is different from the other characters because the narrator gives the reader detailed information about him in the "flashbacks" which are printed in italics.
   → White Mike's thoughts are presented in greater detail compared to the other characters and is the only one who thinks beyond shallow needs like sex and drugs.

2.4 Rounding off

In den ersten beiden *Components* haben sich die Schülerinnen und Schüler ausführlich mit der Exposition des Romans auseinandergesetzt. Abschließend sollen sie jetzt ihre Leseerfahrungen reflektieren. Hierzu wird in Partnerarbeit ein Dialog geschrieben, der sich morgens auf dem Schulweg oder im Schulbus abspielt. Einer der Dialogpartner hat *part I* gelesen und erzählt dem anderen, der das Buch nicht kennt, davon. Wichtig ist, dass nicht nur die Handlung beschrieben, sondern auch die Kapitelstruktur thematisiert wird und dass eine persönliche Bewertung des Gelesenen stattfindet! Um dem Dialog einen entsprechenden Ablauf zu geben, kann der „unwissende" Dialogpartner Fragen stellen, die zu den jeweiligen Punkten führen.

Component 2: Part I (pp. 5–48) – Getting to know the characters – and the book

On their way to school two students talk about *Twelve.* One has read *part I* already, the other hasn't.
With a partner, write a dialogue between those two people in which they talk about the plot, the characters and the structure of the novel. Of course the student who has read part I may state why he/she likes the novel or not!
Make sure that the student who hasn't read the novel asks questions about it in order to create a real dialogue!

In den Dialogen könnte zur Sprache kommen:

- drug dealer who doesn't take drugs himself
- lots of rich kids who live in houses guarded by doormen
- some kids fight during a basketball game
- house party where kids drink alcohol and smoke pot
- one girl uses a new drug called "Twelve"
- strange character "Claude" who buys lots of weapons
- short chapters
- some of them are "flashbacks" and are printed in *italics*
- lots of slang words

Folgende Punkte können bei den Präsentationen der Dialoge schwerpunktmäßig besprochen werden:

Do you agree with what was said about the book?
Did the presenters only read or did they also **act out** their dialogue?

43

Component 3

Part II (pp. 49–96) – Rising action

Nachdem für die Exposition relativ viel Zeit aufgewendet wurde, brennen die Schülerinnen und Schüler nun wahrscheinlich darauf zu erfahren, wie es weitergeht. *Part II* treibt die Handlung voran, indem näher auf die Protagonisten eingegangen wird und Sara Ludlows Plan von der perfekten und legendären Party an Silvester Gestalt annimmt.
Im Laufe von Teil 2 rückt außerdem White Mike weiter in den Mittelpunkt. In zehn *Flashbacks* lernt der Leser immer mehr über ihn. Außerdem wird klar, dass White Mike der Dreh- und Angelpunkt der Handlung ist, da alle Charaktere in irgendeiner Weise mit ihm verbunden sind. Entweder haben sie mit ihm als Dealer zu tun, sind mit ihm verwandt oder befreundet. Für aufmerksame Leser entpuppt sich der *Twelve*-Dealer Lionel als Mörder von Charlie, White Mikes Cousin, sodass White Mike und Lionel noch mehr Verbindungen haben als die rein „geschäftliche". Ziel ist es hier, den Schülerinnen und Schülern zu demonstrieren, das White Mike die zentrale Figur des Romans ist.
Der dritte Schwerpunkt dieses *Components* ist Jessicas Drogenproblem. All ihre Gedanken und Taten drehen sich um *Twelve*, welches sie ab jetzt direkt von Lionel bezieht. Die Thematik wird in einer Art Rollenspiel aufgearbeitet, in dem die Schülerinnen und Schüler die Rolle von Mitarbeitern der Drogenhilfe einnehmen und einen Kongress besuchen, auf dem sie die Wirkungsweisen und Gefahren verschiedener Drogen kennenlernen.

3.1 The action rises – getting into part II

Als Hausaufgabe lesen die Schülerinnen und Schüler *part II* und bearbeiten das entsprechende Arbeitsblatt (*Copy 10* und *Copy 10a*). Auf diese Weise wird das Textverständnis sichergestellt, bevor auf die drei Schwerpunkte des *Components* eingegangen wird.
Bevor das Arbeitsblatt besprochen wird, haben die Schülerinnen und Schüler einige Minuten Zeit, Teil 2 durchzublättern, ihren „Lieblingssatz" zu finden und aufzuschreiben. Außerdem notieren sie Gründe für ihre Wahl.

> Take a couple of minutes and flip through *part II* in order to find your favourite sentence!
> Write down this sentence and indicate page and lines.
> Give reasons for your choice.

Jetzt lassen die Schülerinnen und Schüler ihre Hefte offen liegen, um so eine Art „Ausstellung" ihrer Lieblingssätze zu erzeugen. Alle stehen auf und gehen im Klassenzimmer umher, um sich die Lieblingssätze der anderen – und die Begründungen – anzuschauen. Ein Notizzettel hilft dabei, sich besonders gelungene Beispiele zu merken. Im Anschluss wird im Plenum über die „Ausstellungsstücke" gesprochen.

> Which of the sentences in the exhibition did you like best?
> Do you have questions for the student who wrote it down?

Part II – Rising action

1. While reading, make a list of the characters that appear in *part II* who were already introduced in *part I* and those who are new in *part II*.

already introduced in part I	new in part II

2. **True or false?**
   Check whether the statements below are true or false. If false, write a correct statement underneath the false one.

	true	false
Arturo tells the detective that Hunter is innocent.		
Jessica and the girls discuss sex and parties on their way to the ice-skating rink.		
Sean was also injured at the ice-skating rink.		
Sara acts as if she wants to have sex with Chris.		
Molly is a loud and talkative girl.		
Chris's mother has to keep her Christmas presents in the kitchen.		

3. Describe in no more than 30 words what Claude does after the cocktail party.

4. How many *flashbacks* provide further information about White Mike in *part II*?

Part II – Rising action (solutions)

1. While reading, make a list of the characters that appear in *part II* who were already introduced in *part I* and those who are new in *part II*.

already introduced in part I	new in part II
• Arturo • Hunter • White Mike • Jessica • Chris • Sara • Tobias • Claude • Charlie	• Detective • Andrew • Sean • Lionel • Molly • Alice • Marcelle

2. True or false?
   Check whether the statements below are true or false. If false, write a correct statement underneath the false one.

	true	false
Arturo tells the detective that Hunter is innocent. Arturo lies about Hunter and tells the police that Hunter is a racist.		X
Jessica and the girls discuss sex and parties on their way to the ice-skating rink.	X	
Sean was also injured at the ice-skating rink. He got injured in a car accident.		X
Sara acts as if she wants to have sex with Chris.	X	
Molly is a loud and talkative girl. She is "by nature a quiet girl" (p. 80/ll. 14 f.).		X
Chris's mother has to keep her Christmas presents in the kitchen. She has an extra "wrapping room" for her gifts!		X

3. Describe in no more than 30 words what Claude does after the cocktail party.

> He wants to go shopping for more weapons and asks Tobias to go with him. In Chinatown he runs away from Tobias and afterwards buys an Uzi.

4. How many *flashbacks* provide further information about White Mike in *part II*?

All in all there are 10 flashbacks, only nine of which give information about White Mike.

Component 3: Part II (pp. 49–96) – Rising action

Diese Methode erleichtert es möglicherweise einigen Schülerinnen und Schülern, sich zu äußern, da nicht über die eigenen Sätze gesprochen wird und somit die Hemmschwelle gesenkt ist. Außerdem haben sich die Schülerinnen und Schüler zu Beginn der Stunde recht ausführlich mit Teil 2 beschäftigt und ihr Wissen aktiviert. Die Besprechung des Arbeitsblattes (*Copy 10*) kann je nachdem, wie viel Zeit zur Verfügung steht, zunächst in Partnerarbeit und dann im Plenum oder nur im Plenum erfolgen.

3.2 "I'm not a slut!" – Sara's plan to become famous

Sara ist als Figur konstruiert, die arrogant und berechnend ist, also Antipathien beim Leser weckt. Ihre Eitelkeit und Sucht nach Anerkennung sind der Grund, warum die Silvesterparty überhaupt stattfindet. Umso wichtiger ist es sicherzustellen, dass die Schülerinnen und Schüler Saras Absichten erkennen und über sie und ihre Pläne sprechen.

Zuerst sollen die Schülerinnen und Schüler Fragen vorbereiten, die sie Sara gerne stellen würden, bzw. Aussagen, mit denen sie sie gerne konfrontieren würden. Anschließend bilden alle Schülerinnen und Schüler des Kurses – bis auf eine/n Freiwillige/n – eine Gasse im Klassenzimmer. Der/die Freiwillige schlüpft in die Rolle von Sara und geht durch die Gasse. Die Umstehenden stellen nun ihre Fragen bzw. machen ihre Bemerkungen. „Sara" geht nur weiter und nimmt die Fragen und Aussagen hin. Im anschließenden Gespräch soll der/die Freiwillige sich darüber äußern, wie er/sie sich in Saras Rolle gefühlt hat. Es ist ganz wichtig, dass sich sowohl „Sara" als auch die anderen völlig im Klaren darüber sind, dass sie nur eine Rolle spielt, da die Fragen und Aussagen teilweise sehr hart ausfallen könnten! Im Unterrichtsgespräch soll auf Saras Ziel, berühmt (und berüchtigt) zu werden, hingelenkt werden. Natürlich steht die Art und Weise, wie sie das Ziel erreichen will, im Mittelpunkt.

> How did you feel, walking through the alley as Sara?
> How do you think Sara might have reacted?
> Why did you ask your questions/make your statements?
> What is Sara's goal and how does she try to achieve it?
> Comment on her behaviour.

Ein Tafelbild zur Ergebnissicherung könnte so aussehen:

Sara Ludlow – Her plan to become famous

Sara's ultimate goal: she wants to become famous by throwing a legendary New Year's Eve Party.
Sara's problem: she can't host the party at her own house, as there is always somebody there.
Sara's solution: Chris – he already had a party on Friday, December 27 and his parents will still be out of town on New Year's Eve!
Another problem: Chris doesn't really want another party as he doesn't want anything to get broken in the house.
Sara's solution: She uses her beauty and sex appeal to talk Chris into throwing the party with many more guests than the first party. She even drops hints at having sex with him at the party although she is not interested in Chris at all! Chris is just a means to an end!

→ **Chris can neither resist Sara's charm nor refuse her plans!**
→ **The shallowness of her goal and her selfishness make her a dislikeable character!**

3.3 White Mike – The linchpin of the plot

White Mike ist der Dreh- und Angelpunkt des Plots. Letztendlich laufen alle Fäden bei ihm zusammen, er ist es schließlich auch, der durch seinen „Ausraster" das Massaker an Silvester auslöst. Deshalb ist es jetzt schon wichtig, White Mikes Rolle darzustellen und ihn genauer zu beleuchten. Da noch nicht alle Figuren eingeführt sind, wird hier lediglich festgehalten, dass White Mike die meisten Figuren kennt und mit ihnen zu tun hat. In *Component 6* wird dann eine detaillierte Figurenkonstellation erstellt. Vorbereitend gehen die Schülerinnen und Schüler zu Hause die Kapitel mit White Mike durch und erweitern ihre Mindmap.
Die Besprechung der Hausaufgabe erfolgt in Gruppenarbeit:

> Compare your mind maps and discuss what you found out about White Mike.
> Copy missing information into your mind maps.
> After five minutes each group sends out a spy who looks at the other groups' results in order to inform their group about them.

Schon in dieser frühen Phase des Romans wird deutlich, dass White Mike eine viel komplexere Figur ist als die anderen. Hier bietet es sich an, kurz zu wiederholen, was in *Component 2* in dem Kapitel „The Point of view" (2.3, S. 42) festgehalten wurde:

> The narrator treats White Mike differently than the other characters. Do you remember how he does this?

Um auf den nächsten Schritt überzuleiten, wird jetzt darauf hingewiesen, dass White Mike sich nicht nur durch die *Flashbacks* von den anderen Figuren unterscheidet, sondern auch dadurch, dass er die meisten anderen Figuren kennt, auch solche, die sich gegenseitig nicht kennen. Er ist also eine Art Verbindungsglied, wenn nicht der „linchpin", also der Dreh- und Angelpunkt des Romans. Die beiden entscheidenden Kategorien in der Mindmap sind hier „friends and family" und „customers". Diese Kategorien sollen jetzt mit der Liste der Figuren auf *Copy 10* verglichen werden. Die Schüler sollen diesen Vergleich in Partnerarbeit machen, wobei „friends and family" und „customers" mit jeweils unterschiedlichen Farben auf *Copy 10* unterstrichen werden sollen. Jetzt sucht sich jedes Paar zwei Figuren aus der gleichen Kategorie aus, um diese beiden Figuren in einem Rollenspiel zusammenzuführen.

In diesem Rollenspiel unterhalten sie sich über White Mike. Je nach Konstellation können White Mikes Macken oder auch seine Vorzüge im Mittelpunkt stehen.
Es soll sich hier bewusst nicht um einen vorgeschriebenen Dialog handeln, sondern die Schülerinnen und Schüler sollen nur mit Stichwörtern arbeiten und möglichst frei reden. Versierte Schauspielerinnen bzw. Schauspieler können sogar improvisieren. Damit alle Paare die Möglichkeit haben, ihr Rollenspiel vorzutragen, werden Vorführungsgruppen mit jeweils drei oder vier Paaren gebildet. Diese wiederum bestimmen das Paar, das am Ende im Plenum spielen darf. Durch die verschiedenen Konstellationen konnte White Mike von vielen Seiten beleuchtet werden.

> With a partner, choose two characters from either "friends and family" or "customers" and make them meet and talk about White Mike.
> Imagine what they might say about him in this dialogue and write down keywords.
> Do not write down every single word of the dialogue, but try and speak freely with the help of the keywords.

Mögliche Beobachtungsschwerpunkte für das Publikum während der Vorführungen sind:

> Do the dialogues sound realistic to you?
> What would you have added if you had chosen these characters?
> How was the acting?

Nachdem White Mike jetzt von vielen Seiten beleuchtet wurde, sichert folgendes Tafelbild die Erkenntnis, dass White Mike eine besondere Rolle innehat:

White Mike revisited

White Mike is a special character, because …
1. … the omniscient narrator pays special attention to him.
2. … he knows most of the characters in the novel (and is known by them).

→ White Mike is the **linchpin** of the plot, because he is part of all the different sub-plots of the novel!

3.4 Jessica – the drug victim

Drogen sind ein zentraler Bestandteil im Leben der Jugendlichen im Roman *Twelve*. Umso wichtiger ist es, dieses Thema gezielt mit den Schülerinnen und Schülern zu bearbeiten. Aus dem Unterricht der Mittelstufe sollten die Schülerinnen und Schüler Vorkenntnisse besitzen, die hier eingebracht werden können. Es sollte unbedingt problematisiert werden, mit welcher Selbstverständlichkeit die Jugendlichen in *Twelve* Drogen konsumieren und wie zentral diese für die Alltagsgestaltung sind. Zuerst wird daher die Aufmerksamkeit auf die Omnipräsenz von Drogen in *Twelve* gelenkt, indem die Schülerinnen und Schüler *Copy 11* bearbeiten (Lösungen auf *Copy 11a*). Hier wird deutlich, dass die meisten Figuren Drogen konsumieren und dass Drogen, v.a. Marihuana, zentraler Bestandteil des Lebens der Jugendlichen der Upper East Side sind. Außerdem wird die Droge *Twelve* unter die Lupe genommen und damit natürlich auch Jessica, die im Roman die einzige Konsumentin dieser neuen Droge ist, die offensichtlich hochwirksam und stark süchtig macht. Bei Jessica macht sich schon nach zwei Tagen eine Wesensänderung bemerkbar. Diese schnelle „Drogenkarriere" sollen die Schülerinnen und Schüler jetzt in einem Schreibauftrag nachzeichnen. Die Bearbeitung der Drogenproblematik erfolgt in einer Art Rollenspiel, in dem die Schülerinnen und Schüler Mitarbeiter der Drogenhilfe darstellen und sich auf einem Kongress weiterbilden. Im Anschluss versuchen sie, Jessica direkt Hilfe zu leisten.

> Imagine you are a volunteer at a drug rehab center. On the basis of the last table on *Copy 11* write a report about Jessica's behaviour for your files. What kind of girl is she? How has she changed because of her drug abuse?

Nach dieser Auseinandersetzung mit der Droge und ihren Wirkungen wird jetzt in Gruppenarbeit ein Kurzvortrag erarbeitet, der auf einem Kongress für Mitarbeiter der Drogenhilfe gehalten werden soll.

Drugs in Nick McDonell's *Twelve*

Drugs play a central part in the lives of the kids in *Twelve*. Therefore, it is important to take a close look at this phenomenon and how it is described in the novel.

1. White Mike sells drugs for a living. Which drug is his main source of income?
   _____

2. Which other drugs have been mentioned in the novel so far?
   _____

3. Who actually takes drugs in *Twelve?* Give examples. Does the text say which drugs they use? Don't forget to write down where you found the information.
   _____
   _____
   _____
   _____
   _____

4. *Twelve* is a designer drug that only exists in this novel. What are the drug's effects as described in the book?

5. Reread chapters 10, 24, 26, and 37 and make a "before and after" comparison of Jessica.

Before 12	After 12

Drugs in Nick McDonell's *Twelve* (solutions)

Drugs play a central part in the lives of the kids in *Twelve*. Therefore, it is important to take a close look at this phenomenon and how it is described in the novel.

1. White Mike sells drugs for a living. Which drug is his main source of income?

marijuana

2. Other drugs have been mentioned so far. Which ones? Where are they mentioned?

cocaine (e.g. p. 33, l. 13), Twelve (e.g. p. 33, l. 19), ecstasy (p. 57, l. 26), crack (p. 67, l. 12)

3. Who actually takes drugs in *Twelve*? Give examples. Does the text say which drugs they use? Don't forget to write down where you found the information.

Claude: marijuana (p. 37, l. 4), used to do cocaine (p. 38, l. 9), **Jessica:** cocaine (actually thinks she is doing cocaine when she first tries Twelve on p. 33, ll. 14 ff.), Twelve (ibd.; p. 91, ll. 20 ff.), Ecstasy (p. 57, l. 26) **Chris:** marijuana (p. 89, l. 19), **Charlie:** no specific drug mentioned (p. 73, ll. 11 f.), **some kids at Chris's party:** marijuana (p. 30, l. 16), **Tobias:** marijuana (p. 93, ll. 16 ff.), **Alice:** marijuana (p. 92, l. 17)

4. *Twelve* is a designer drug that only exists in this novel. What are the drug's effects as described in the book?

On pp. 33 ff. the effects are described: tingling down the spine, muscle tension, Jessica grins involuntarily, she starts sweating, she sees dancing colours, she giggles and passes out (*Twelve* seems to be a very potent drug).

5. Reread chapters 10, 24, 26, and 37 and make a "before and after" comparison of Jessica.

Before 12	After 12
• healthy-looking, athletic (p. 32, l. 16) • very good student (p. 34, ll. 3 ff.) • self-confident (p. 33, l. 4) • gets drugs from friends (p. 33, l. 19)	• wants to buy *Twelve* directly from White Mike (p. 57, ll. 15 ff.) • nervous, especially when thinking about *Twelve* (p. 57, ll. 27 f.) • not self-confident during the deal (pp. 68 f.) • *Twelve* the only thing she can think about (p. 74, ll. 3 f.) • loses control of her consumption (p. 91, ll. 20 ff.)

> You are still a member of staff at the rehab center. Your boss asks you to give a little speech about the use, effects and dangers of Twelve at a convention of drug experts. Use *Copy 11* and your report as a basis for your work.
> Come up with one master version to present in class.

Der vorherige Schreibauftrag wird auf diese Weise zwar nicht explizit besprochen, die Ergebnisse können aber von allen in die Gruppenarbeit mit eingebracht werden. Falls es an der Schule ein Rednerpult gibt, bietet es sich an, dieses für die Vorträge der Ergebnisse ins Klassenzimmer mitzubringen und die Tische auf die Seite zu stellen, sodass reine Stuhlreihen entstehen, wie in einem Vortragsraum. Die vortragenden Schülerinnen und Schüler sprechen in ihrer Funktion/Rolle als Mitarbeiter der Drogenhilfe und nicht als sie selbst! Welches Gruppenmitglied den ausgearbeiteten Vortrag tatsächlich hält, kann von der Lehrkraft bestimmt, ausgelost oder von den Gruppen selbst bestimmt werden.

Nach den Vorträgen wird weiter im Rahmen des Kongresses gearbeitet. In verschiedenen Workshops werden Informationen über verschiedene Drogen im Internet gesucht (s. *Copy 12*). *Ecstasy* wurde hier mit aufgenommen, da Jessica *Twelve* mit *Ecstasy* vergleicht. Je nach Zeitbudget kann die Recherche vorbereitend zu Hause oder in Gruppen während des Unterrichts erfolgen. Die Infoposter werden in jedem Fall während des Unterrichts erstellt. Um Eintönigkeit zu vermeiden, sollten die vorherigen Gruppen aufgelöst und neue gebildet werden. Auf dem Arbeitsblatt stehen Buchstaben vor den Arbeitsaufträgen. Jeder Gruppe muss also ein Buchstabe zugeordnet werden. Je nach Klassengröße müssen u. U. mehrere Gruppen das gleiche Thema bearbeiten, deshalb pro Arbeitsauftrag zwei Buchstaben.

> At the meeting there are different workshops that help the volunteers learn more about different drugs, their effects and dangers.
> Form new groups in order to do some Internet research according to the instructions on *Copy 12*.
> Each group will be assigned a letter so that you know which topic you are supposed to work on.

Auf dem Arbeitsblatt sind *starting points* im Internet angegeben, von denen aus die Gruppen ihre Informationen sammeln sollen. Es ist nicht nur sinnvoll, die Schülerinnen und Schüler hier starten zu lassen, um die Recherche effektiver zu gestalten, sondern auch, um zu vermeiden, dass u. U. auf Seiten recherchiert wird, die Drogenkonsum befürworten! Vor der Präsentation der Ergebnisse sollten die Vortragenden wieder darauf hingewiesen werden, dass sie in ihrer Rolle als Mitarbeiter der Drogenhilfe sprechen. Zur Ergebnissicherung können die Poster fotografiert und anschließend für alle kopiert oder digital zur Verfügung gestellt werden. Alternativ können die Gruppen ein Handout erstellen.

Zum Abschluss des Kongresses sollen alle Schülerinnen und Schüler einen Brief an Jessica verfassen, in dem sie ihre Lage analysieren und Empfehlungen für die Zukunft geben:

> After the meeting you want to help Jessica even more than before. Write a letter to her in which you analyse her behaviour and try to help her find a way out of her addiction!

Eine Möglichkeit, mit den Briefen weiterzuarbeiten, ist, sie in Partnerarbeit auszutauschen; jeder soll eine Antwort aus Jessicas Sicht schreiben. Alternativ können auch einige Briefe im Plenum vorgelesen und mögliche Reaktionen Jessicas im Unterrichtsgespräch diskutiert werden. Auf diese Weise spekulieren die Schülerinnen und Schüler natürlich auch schon über den Fortgang der Handlung – Lust zum Weiterlesen könnte so geweckt werden!

Drug abuse and drug prevention

You are still at the meeting of drug experts and after hearing about Jessica in the speeches you will now go into different workshops to learn more about the drugs that are used in *Twelve*. As the drug *Twelve* does not actually exist, one group will research Ecstasy which is, according to Jessica, quite similar to *Twelve*.

- Find your group according to the letter you've just drawn.
- Log on to the Internet and find information about the drug that is related to your letter below.
- Use the given URL as a starting point to find as many facts as possible.
- Your aim is to come up with an informational poster that you will present in class.
- The poster should give information about use, common and long-term effects, problems, etc. of the specific drug.
- Mention any characters in *Twelve* that use the drug you are talking about!
- You may use some printouts from the Internet if they help you to make your point!

A and D: Find information about marijuana.

→ Start at
http://teens.drugabuse.gov/facts/facts_mj1.php

B and E: Find information about Ecstasy.

→ Start at
http://teens.drugabuse.gov/facts/facts_xtc1.php

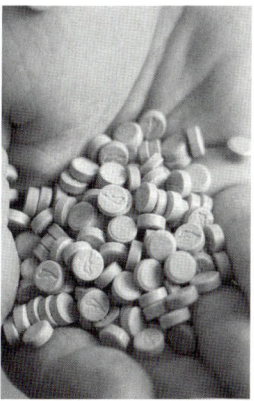

C and F: Find information about so-called stimulants.

→ Start at
http://teens.drugabuse.gov/facts/facts_stim1.php

Your teacher will tell you how much time you have to finish the poster!

Component 4

Music and language in *Twelve*

Nachdem die ersten beiden Teile des Romans besprochen wurden, wird der Fortlauf der Handlung jetzt unterbrochen, um auf die Musik einzugehen, die den Roman prägt und die Handlung wie ein Soundtrack untermalt. Außerdem wird die Sprache behandelt, die oft umgangssprachlich und teilweise auch vulgär ist. Nick McDonell schreibt so, wie die jugendlichen Protagonisten reden, was dem Text Authentizität verleiht.

Component 4 beginnt damit, ein Bewusstsein für die Funktion von Musik im Film zu schaffen. Danach werden drei Lieder und die dazugehörigen Szenen in Teil 1 genauer beleuchtet, um zu zeigen, dass die Lieder in *Twelve* die gleiche Funktion erfüllen können. Die Arbeit mit den Liedern bietet die Möglichkeit, Lexik zu behandeln, die nicht explizit im Buch vorkommt.

Im Anschluss an den Soundtrack wird die Sprache beleuchtet. Nachdem verschiedene Kapitel nach umgangssprachlichen und anstößigen Wendungen und Wörtern durchsucht wurden, wird auf den unterschiedlichen Gebrauch von Sprache in unterschiedlichen Situationen eingegangen, um zu verdeutlichen, warum Nick McDonell neben schriftsprachlichen so viele umgangssprachliche Elemente im Roman verwendet. Die Schülerinnen und Schüler sollen den Zusammenhang zwischen Sprachstil und Erzählperspektive herausfinden.

Der *Component* schließt mit Kopiervorlagen für Lernvokabular sowohl aus den einzelnen Teilen des Romans als auch aus den Liedern, die in Kapitel 4.1 behandelt werden (*Copies 17–22*, S. 64–69).

4.1 The songs in parts I and II

Musik ist ein zentraler Bestandteil im Leben von Jugendlichen. Auch in *Twelve* wird Musik thematisiert. Drei Lieder wurden schon auf *Copy 8* erwähnt, jetzt sollen diese jedoch detaillierter besprochen werden. Zunächst wird verdeutlicht, wie wichtig Musik für die Schaffung von Atmosphäre in Filmen ist. Wenn der Leser die Lieder kennt, die in *Twelve* vorkommen, erfüllen diese im Roman die gleiche Funktion. Im Prinzip kann die Funktion von Musik im Film anhand jedes beliebigen Films demonstriert werden. Die Lehrkraft kann wahlweise eine rasante Actionszene oder eine ruhige und romantische Filmepisode zur Veranschaulichung nutzen.

What function does music have in films?
Can you remember movies/certain scenes in movies where music is particularly important?

Jetzt wird die von der Lehrkraft ausgewählte Filmszene wahlweise mit Bild und ohne Ton oder umgekehrt vorgespielt. Die Schülerinnen und Schüler formulieren ihre Erwartungen an die Musik bzw. an den Film schriftlich. Außerdem schreiben sie auf, ob sie den Film bereits kennen oder ob sie die Szene/die Musik an einen Film erinnert, den sie bereits kennen.

As you listen to the music/watch the scene, write down what you expect the pictures/the music to be like.
Do you know the movie or does the music/the scene remind you of a movie?

> Before we talk in class about what you've written down, check some of your classmates' predictions and talk about them.

Nach dem anschließenden Unterrichtsgespräch, in dem die Schülerinnen und Schüler ihre Erwartungen mitteilen, wird die Szene einmal mit Ton/Bild vorgespielt, um zu klären, inwieweit die Erwartungen der Wirklichkeit der gegebenen Filmszene entsprechen.
Folgendes Tafelbild, das später erweitert wird, schließt diese Phase ab:

Twelve – a novel with a soundtrack

In films, music supports what is seen on the screen.
It helps the filmmaker to create the atmosphere he or she wants to establish, e.g. an action thriller or a romantic drama.

In einer arbeitsteiligen Gruppenarbeit werden jetzt die drei Lieder aus *part I* bearbeitet; dabei werden nicht nur die Texte, sondern auch die Künstler und die Funktion der Lieder im Buch untersucht. Die Materialien für die einzelnen Gruppen finden sich auf **Copies 13–15**.
Für die Arbeit sollten den Schülerinnen und Schülern Wörterbücher zur Verfügung gestellt werden. Alternativ kann das Internet genutzt werden, um Informationen zu den Liedern und zu den Künstlern zu recherchieren.
Natürlich bietet es sich auch an, den Schülerinnen und Schülern die Lieder auf einem Tonträger zur Verfügung zu stellen, damit sie auch angehört werden können. James Taylors *Fire and rain* erschien erstmals auf dem Album *Sweet Baby James* (Warner Bros., 1970), Ben Harpers *Burn one down* auf dem Album *Fight for your Mind* (EMI, 1995) und Nellys *Ride wit me* auf dem Album *Country Grammar* (Universal, 2000). Die genannten Titel sind z. B. auf „iTunes" oder „musicload.de" (auch einzeln) als Download erhältlich.
Falls nur wenig Zeit zur Verfügung steht, können sich die Präsentationen nur auf die Lieder beschränken, die biografischen Aspekte der Künstler werden weggelassen.

> In groups, work on the following tasks and come up with a poster to introduce your song and the singer:
> - Give some information about the singer.
> - What is your song about?
> - Describe the sound of the song.
> - Where does it appear in *Twelve*?
> - What atmosphere does it create in the novel?

Je nach Klassengröße müssen evtl. mehrere Gruppen das gleiche Lied bearbeiten und die Lehrkraft muss abwägen, ob alle Gruppen ihre Ergebnisse vortragen. Falls die Zeit dies nicht zulässt, sollten diejenigen, die nicht zum Zug kommen, dazu animiert werden, Ergänzungen vorzuschlagen. Falls die Lieder zur Verfügung stehen, sollten sie vor den Präsentationen angespielt werden. Mit den Ergebnissen der Gruppenarbeit wird das obige Tafelbild ergänzt:

Twelve – a novel with a soundtrack

In films, music supports what is seen on the screen.
It helps the filmmaker to create the atmosphere he or she wants to establish, e.g. an action thriller or a romantic drama.

Likewise, music plays a decisive role for the atmosphere in *Twelve*. Knowing the songs that occur in parts I and II helps readers to create a soundtrack in their minds while reading.

- James Taylor's *Fire and Rain* is a sad song that – if at all – "tough" kids like Hunter only listen to in secret.
- Nelly's *Ride wit me* is a rap song about fame, money, parties and girls and is played at Chris's party. The line "must be the money" is an allusion to the wealth of the Upper East Side.
- Ben Harper's *Burn one down* is a hymn for people who smoke marijuana. The potheads at Chris's party listen to this acoustic song while smoking on the terrace.

James Taylor: *Fire and rain*

Summary

James Taylor wrote this song as a reaction to the suicide of a close friend, Suzanne Schnerr. In the beginning of the song he talks about his aimlessness after having learned about the suicide. He walks around and finally comes up with this song.

While further reflecting life and death he sings about good times and sunny days that he thought would never end, which the "fire" in the title stands for. In direct opposition stands the "rain" which represents lonely times in James Taylor's life. In these times he was so alone that he couldn't even find any friends. The only anchor he had in those times was the thought he might meet Suzanne again some time! Now he's so desperate that he even asks Jesus for some help in his life, which is typical for people feeling desperate and lonely. During th sunny days he probably didn't so much as to even think about Jesus or religion.

The song's overall mood is very sad and contemplative which is supported by calm and slow music.

James Taylor – biography

The American singer and songwriter James Taylor was born on March 12, 1948 in Boston, Massachusetts into a wealthy family. His mother was a trained soprano singer and encouraged young James to play several instruments. As a teenager he started to cause trouble and, when he was 15, his parents sent him to a boarding school which he never graduated from. Soon he suffered from major depression and slid into a heroin addiction at the age of 18. With his band "Flying Machine" (cf. lyrics of *Fire and rain*: "flying machines in pieces on the ground") he played music in London, but they failed to become successful. In 1969 he returned to the US and went to rehab. Finally drug-free, he recorded *Fire and rain*. The song, in which he sings about his fears and problems, was inspired by his own experiences in psychiatric institutions and the suicide of a close friend (Suzanne Schnerr). *Fire and rain* became one of his greatest hits and was part of his album *Sweet Baby James* which sold more than two million copies in 1970.

The early 1970s were his most successful years, during which he won several Grammy Awards. He experienced troubled times during the 1980s and early 1990s, including a divorce and several other setbacks. In 1997 he had a successful comeback with the album Hourglass. James Taylor is still active in the music business and released his most recent studio album *One Man Band* in 2007.

His charity work includes support of the Rainforest Foundation Fund.

Nelly: *Ride wit me*

Lyrics (chorus and first verse)

If you wanna go and take a ride wit me
With three-wheelin in the fo' with the gold D's
Oh why do I live this way? (Hey, must be the money!)

If you wanna go and get high wit me
5 Smoke a L in the back of the Benz-y
Oh why must I feel this way? (Hey, must be the money!)

In the club on the late night, feelin right
Lookin tryin to spot somethin real nice
Lookin for a little shorty hot and horny so that I can take home (I can take home)
10 She can be 18 (18) wit an attitude
or 19 kinda snotty actin real rude
Boo, as long as you a thicky thicky thick girl
you know that it's on (Know that it's on)
I peep something comin towards me up the dance floor, Sexy and real slow (hey)
15 Sayin she was peepin and I dig the last video
So when Nelly, can we go; how could I tell her no?
Her measurements were 36-25-34
Yellin I like the way you brush your hair
And I like those stylish clothes you wear
20 I like the way the light hit the ice and glare
And I can see you moving way over there

three-wheelin' driving on three wheels
fo' special car (1964 Chevrolet Impala)
D's rims (*Felgen*); short for "Daytonas"

Musik: Eldra P. DeBarge/William Randall DeBarge/Jordan Etterlane/Cornell Haynes/Jason Epperson
Text: Eldra P. DeBarge/William Randall DeBarge/Jordan Etterlane/Cornell Haynes © 1982 by Jobete Music Co. Inc.
Rechte für Deutschland, Österreich, Schweiz und Osteuropa (außer Baltikum): EMI Songs Musikverlag GmbH, Hamburg

Nelly – biography

The American Rap artist Nelly was born Cornell Haynes Jr. on November 2, 1974 in St. Louis, Missouri. His father was an officer in the Air Force and Nelly spent three of his childhood years in Spain. Facing serious financial problems, his parents got divorced when Nelly was eight. As a teenager he mostly hung around with friends and got into trouble, and he was moved around to several different family members.

Finally he started playing baseball and was really successful, which helped him stay out of trouble. Nelly was such a good baseball player that he planned to become a professional. During his time in an amateur league he started a rap band called *St. Lunatics* and recorded some songs which sold quite well in the St. Louis area.

After *St. Lunatics* tried their luck in Atlanta, they realized that Nelly might be more successful as a solo artist. His first solo album *Country Grammar* hit number one in the Billboard charts in 2000 (beating Britney and Eminem), and it became clear that Nelly wouldn't play baseball anymore.

Nelly's big advantage was that he didn't fit into any given rap scene: He was neither "West Coast" nor "East Coast" and wasn't part of the "Dirty South", which made him a universal rapper from the American Midwest.

In 2008 he released his eighth solo album *Brass Knuckles*.

His charity work includes campaigning for disabled kids as well as for bone marrow donation to help cancer patients.

Ben Harper: *Burn one down*

Lyrics

Let us burn one from end to end,
And pass it over to me my friend.
Burn it long, we'll burn it slow,
To light me up before I go.

5 If you don't like my fire, then don't come around,
'cause I'm gonna burn one down.
Yes, I'm gonna burn one down.

My choice is what I choose to do,
And if I'm causing no harm,
10 it shouldn't bother you.

Your choice is who you choose to be,
And if you're causin' no harm,
then you're alright with me.

If you don't like my fire, then don't come around,
15 'cause I'm gonna burn one down.
Yes, I'm gonna burn one down.

Herb the gift from the earth,
And what's from the earth is of the greatest worth.
So before you knock it try it first,
20 Oh, you'll see it's a blessing and not a curse.

If you don't like my fire, then don't come around,
'cause I'm gonna burn one down.
Yes, I'm gonna burn one, oohhh.

Musik und Text: Ben Harper © 1995 by Innocent Criminal/EMI Virgin Music Inc. Rechte für Deutschland, Österreich, Schweiz und Osteuropa (außer Baltikum): EMI Virgin Music Publishing Germany GmbH, Hamburg

Ben Harper – biography

The American singer, songwriter and guitarist Ben Harper was born Benjamin Chase Harper on October 28, 1969 in Pomona, California. Ben's family background is multi-ethnic as his father has African-American and Cherokee ancestors and his mother is Jewish. His parents both played music, and Ben started playing the guitar at a young age.
When he was five, his parents were divorced and he and his two brothers lived with his mother.
In 1977 he attended a Bob Marley show which is said to have been a deep inspiration for him. He started performing publicly when he was twelve, his influences being blues, folk, reggae and R'n'B.
In 1992 he released his first album *Pleasure and Pain*. His breakthrough, however, was his third album *Fight for your Mind* which was released in 1995 and was certificated gold. Three more of his 13 albums have been certificated gold so far. Furthermore, he received two Grammy Awards in 2005.
In 1999 he met Jack Johnson at a concert. They became friends and Ben gave Jack's demo tape to his producer who recorded Jack's first CD in early 2001.
From 1996 to 2001 Ben was married to Joanna, with whom he has two children. He also has two children with Laura Dern, whom he married in 2005.
His charity work includes support for Amnesty International, women's rights and environmental projects (e.g. against nuclear power).

4.2 Parental advisory – explicit language!

Als Einstieg in die nähere Untersuchung der Sprache in *Twelve* suchen die Schülerinnen und Schüler als Hausaufgabe im Internet Informationen über das Logo *Parental Advisory – Explicit Content*. Dazu schreibt die Lehrkraft den Titel dieses Logos an die Tafel. Vielen Schülerinnen und Schülern ist diese Phrase von CDs oder DVDs bekannt. Die *Recording Industry Association of America* (RIAA) führte einen entsprechenden Aufkleber 1985 ein, um auf anstößige Inhalte von Tonträgern hinzuweisen. Alternativ kann auch gleich ein Unterrichtsgespräch geführt werden:

> Have you read these words before?
> Where have you read them?
> What is it about?

Es soll hier jedoch nicht nur um anstößige Wörter gehen, sondern um Umgangssprache im Allgemeinen, die *Twelve* von vielen anderen Romanen unterscheidet. In Partnerarbeit bearbeiten die Schülerinnen und Schüler jetzt **Copy 16** (Lösungen auf **Copy 16a**), um umgangssprachliche Wörter und Wendungen zu finden. Dieser Sprachgebrauch interessiert die Schülerinnen und Schüler besonders, da er normalerweise nicht Gegenstand des Englischunterrichts ist. Bei der Besprechung der Ergebnisse muss nicht auf jede der genannten Passagen eingegangen werden, da es vor allem auf die Sensibilisierung für die Sprache und weniger auf Vollständigkeit ankommt.

Allerdings schreibt Nick McDonell nicht nur in Umgangssprache. Im Gegenteil: Weite Strecken des Romans sind schriftsprachlich, teilweise sogar bildungssprachlich (z. B. S. 67, Z. 17 *cognizant*) geprägt. Je nach Perspektive, die der Erzähler einnimmt, ändert sich auch die Sprache. Wörtliche Rede ist meist umgangssprachlich gehalten. Um zu verdeutlichen, dass Sprache in unterschiedlichen Situationen auch unterschiedlich gebraucht wird, sollen die Schülerinnen und Schüler aufschreiben, wie sie verschiedene Menschen von unterschiedlichem Status darum bitten würden, ihnen einen Gegenstand, z. B. einen Stift, zu geben.

> Imagine that you want somebody to give you a pen. Write down how you would ask for it from
> - your younger brother,
> - your best friend,
> - your father,
> - your teacher.
>
> Mögliche Lösungen:
> - younger brother: "Gimme the pen!"
> - best friend: "Can I have the pen?"
> - father: "Can you give me the pen, please?"
> - teacher: "Would you please give me the pen, sir/ma'am?"

Im folgenden Unterrichtsgespräch soll vor diesem Hintergrund die Verbindung zwischen Erzählperspektive und Sprachgebrauch hergestellt werden. Dazu wird zunächst kurz die Erzählperspektive in *Twelve* wiederholt, um dann zu besprechen, wann eher umgangssprachlich und wann eher schriftsprachlich geschrieben wird.

> What kind of narrator tells the story of *Twelve*?
> Whose perspective does the third-person narrator take?
> You used different styles of language to ask for a pen. Does the narrator also use different styles in different situations?
> What effect does this have?

Das entsprechende Tafelbild zur Ergebnissicherung:

> **The use of language in *Twelve***
>
> Nick McDonell uses many colloquial expressions (e.g. gimme, 'em, you know, like, etc.) and explicit language (e.g. shit, fuck, dick, etc.).
> → This makes *Twelve* different from many other novels.
>
> BUT: There are also parts in which the author makes use of literary language.
> → The language style used in *Twelve* depends on the situation and the point of view the narrator takes.
> → Some characters make more (e.g. Arturo) and some make less (e.g. White Mike) use of slang.
> → Dialogues have a colloquial tone.
> → Language contributes to the credibility and atmosphere of the novel.

Abschließend stellt sich die Frage, ob ein *Parental Advisory*-Aufkleber auf dem Cover von *Twelve* gerechtfertigt wäre. Die Schülerinnen und Schüler sollen dies schriftlich erörtern. Je nach Kenntnisstand der Klasse können entsprechende formale und lexikalische Kriterien für Erörterungen eingeführt bzw. wiederholt werden.

> If you were a member of an organization for the protection of minors (Jugendschutz), would you argue for a sticker *Parental Advisory – Explicit Content* on the cover of *Twelve*? Give reasons for and against such an action.

Colloquial and explicit language in *Twelve*

Twelve is full of slang expressions and explicit language. With a partner, check the following sections of *part I and II* and write down examples. One partner checks the even numbers, the other checks the odd ones. Always indicate the page and line(s) where the words and expressions are found.

section	expressions that are slang and/or explicit
Chapter 1 (White Mike is introduced)	
Chapter 2 (Hunter at the Rec)	
Chapter 6 (Lionel and Charlie)	
Chapter 16 (Arturo talks to police detective)	
Chapter 18 (Jessica and her girls)	
Chapter 19 (Chris and Jessica on the phone)	
Chapter 23 (Lionel and White Mike)	
Chapter 30 (Molly at the agency)	
Chapter 36 (Chris and Claude at the cocktail party)	

Now tell your partner about your findings and write down what your partner has found out.

Colloquial and explicit language in *Twelve* (solutions)

Twelve is full of slang expressions and explicit language. With a partner, check the following sections of *part I and II* and write down examples. One partner checks the even numbers, the other checks the odd ones. Always indicate the page and line(s) where the words and expressions are found.

section	expressions that are slang and/or explicit
Chapter 1 (White Mike is introduced)	fuck that (p. 6/l. 5); frozen dog shit (p. 7, l. 4)
Chapter 2 (Hunter at the Rec)	gimme my fuckin' spot back (p. 12, l. 12); Hunter is pissed (p. 14, l. 19); kick the nigger's ass some more (p. 15, l. 1); Hunter tells him to get the fuck away (p. 15, l. 2); he calls Hunter a pussy (p. 15, ll. 3 f.)
Chapter 6 (Lionel and Charlie)	fuckin' guy (p. 23, l. 1); scary pissed (p. 23, l. 2); gimme the money (p. 23, l. 5)
Chapter 16 (Arturo talks to police detective)	punk kid (p. 49, l. 19); fuckin' with him (p. 49, l. 20); one of them Nazis (p. 49, l. 21); broke 'em up (p. 50, l. 2); looking out for my boy (p. 50, l. 4); yeah, man (p. 50, l. 9)
Chapter 18 (Jessica and her girls)	really shitty (p. 54, l. 20); give blow jobs (p. 55, l. 3); until, like, the time is right (p. 55, l. 4); chicks must come before dicks (p. 55, l. 6); parents suck (p. 55, l. 9); even though, like, I tell my mom everything, but not everything everything, you know? (p. 55, ll. 9 ff.); like, like, like, ... (p. 55, l. 24)
Chapter 19 (Chris and Jessica on the phone)	totally freaked out (p. 56, l. 20); sure, yeah (p. 57, l. 6); didn't try to fuck her (p. 57, l. 7); You get your weed from that White Mike guy, right? (p. 57, ll. 15 f.); wanna get some (p. 57, l. 19); coke (p. 57, l. 21); it fucked Claude up (p. 57, l. 22)
Chapter 23 (Lionel and White Mike)	creepy dude (p. 67, l. 1); gonna shoot you (p. 68, l. 1); bitch, bitch-ass nigger fucks with me, cop, punk-kid (p. 68, ll. 3 ff.)
Chapter 30 (Molly at the agency)	keep 'em guessing (p. 80, l. 8); the land of assholes (p. 80, l. 13); jerks (p. 80, l. 19); no kidding (p. 80, l. 22)
Chapter 36 (Chris and Claude at the cocktail party)	feels weird (p. 89, l. 21); what the fuck (p. 89, l. 22); hip (p. 90, l. 19); Oh, you know, everything (p. 91, l. 3); you know (p. 91, ll. 10 f.); you a Beatles fan (p. 91, l. 17); fuck the Beatles (p. 91, l. 19)

Now tell your partner about your findings and write down what your partner has found out.

Study vocab part I

Literary terms

main character	*Hauptperson*	main character = protagonist
setting	*Schauplatz, Setting*	the setting of a story consists of time and place
exposition	*Exposition, Einleitung*	adj.: expository
narrator	*Erzähler*	
point of view	*Erzählperspektive*	The point of view in *Twelve* is that of an omniscient third-person narrator
omniscient	*allwissend*	

Eating disorders

eating disorder	*Essstörung*	
anorexic	*magersüchtig*	noun: anorexia
skinny	*mager, dürr*	skinny ↔ fat
bulimic	*bulimisch*	noun: bulimia = *Ess-Brech-Sucht*
(to) conceal sth.	*etw. verbergen*	concealment = *Verborgenheit*

Body parts

skull	*Schädel*	
temple	*Schläfe*	
forehead	*Stirn*	
spine	*Rückgrat, Wirbelsäule*	
thigh	*Oberschenkel*	
shin	*Schienbein*	
sinew	*Sehne*	sinew = tendon
navel	*Bauchnabel*	navel = belly button

City and school

construction site	*Baustelle*	
concrete	*Beton*	
(housing) project	*Wohnsiedlung mit Sozialwohnungen*	Nana lives in the projects.
gym	*Sporthalle*	
field trip	*Schulausflug*	
boarding school	*Internat*	Many of the rich Upper East Side kids attend private boarding schools.
(to) attend school	*die Schule besuchen*	

Movements

(to) flinch	*zurückzucken*	
(to) back off	*zurückweichen*	
(to) shrug	*mit den Achseln zucken*	
(to) clutch sth	*etw. umklammern*	
(to) hurl sth	*etw. schleudern, werfen*	(to) hurl = (to) toss, (to) throw

Miscellaneous

(to) memorize sth	*sich etw. einprägen*	memory = *Gedächtnis*
stack	*Haufen, Stapel*	stack = pile
(to) peer around	*um sich schauen*	
(to) mutter	*murmeln*	
muffled	*gedämpft*	
split second	*Bruchteil einer Sekunde*	
(to) be out of place	*fehl am Platz sein*	
(to) pass out	*ohnmächtig werden*	(to) pass out = (to) faint
flawless	*makellos*	flaw = *Makel*
devotion	*Hingabe*	(to) be devoted to sth. = *etw. mit Hingabe machen*
(to) dedicate sth to sb	*jmd. etw. widmen*	
(to) rip sth	*etw. zerreißen*	(to) rip = (to) tear
(to) indicate sth	*etw. zu verstehen geben*	
disguised	*getarnt, verkleidet*	
(to) be alert	*auf der Hut sein*	
scary	*unheimlich, Angst machend*	scary = gruesome

Study vocab part II

Literary terms

flashback	*Rückblende*	The flashbacks in *Twelve* are printed in italics.
plot	*Handlung*	
subplot	*Nebenhandlung*	

Around the house

housekeeper	*Haushälter(in)*	
nanny	*Kindermädchen*	All the kids in *Twelve* seem to have had nannies.
stairwell	*Treppenhaus*	
(to) room with sb	*mit jdm. das Zimmer teilen*	
intercom	*Gegensprechanlage*	
counter	*(Küchen-)Arbeitsplatte, Theke*	
tile	*Fliese*	
balcony	*Balkon*	
back porch	*Terrasse*	back porch = patio
duplex	*Doppelhaus*	
estate	*Anwesen*	
blinds	*Jalousien*	(to) draw the blinds = *die Jalousien auf-/zuziehen*

Crime and police

(to) mess with sb	*sich mit jmd. anlegen*	Don't mess with him. He's a kung fu fighter!
rapist	*Vergewaltiger*	verb: (to) rape sb
(to) track sb down	*jmd. ausfindig machen*	
(to) figure sth out	*etw. herausfinden*	
holding cell	*Arrestzelle*	
forensic	*gerichtsmedizinisch*	
private investigator	*Privatdetektiv*	

Money

broke	*pleite*	
(to) pawn sth	*etw. verpfänden*	If you want to pawn sth, you go to a pawn shop.
cash-advance line	*Überziehungskredit*	
checking account	*Bankkonto, Girokonto*	
receipt	*Kassenzettel, Bon*	
greed	*Gier*	greed ↔ generosity

Movements

(to) stroll	*schlendern, bummeln*	(to) stroll around the city
(to) zip up	*mit Reißverschluss schließen*	zipper = *Reißverschluss*
(to) tense	*verkrampfen, sich anspannen*	tension = *Spannung*
(to) strut	*stolzieren*	
(to) squint	*blinzeln*	(to) squint = (to) wink
(to) dart at sth	*blitzschnell auf etw. losschießen*	The fish darted at their prey.
(to) start	*zusammenzucken*	

Miscellaneous

distracted	*verwirrt, zerstreut*	distracted ↔ focused, concentrated
sparse	*spärlich, dünn*	Chris has sparse armpit hair.
(to) trade on sth	*sich etw. zunutze machen*	
incredible	*unglaublich*	Sara is incredibly beautiful.
uneasy	*unwohl, unbehaglich*	
weird	*seltsam, eigenartig*	
(to) come off as naïve	*naiv wirken*	
imperceptible	*unmerklich, nicht wahrnehmbar*	(to) perceive sth = *etw. wahrnehmen*
highlighter	*Leuchtstift*	verb: (to) highlight sth
(to) mourn sb	*um jdn. trauern*	
worn out	*abgenutzt, stark gebraucht*	worn out ↔ brand new
(to) run into sb	*jdn. unvermittelt treffen*	
alley	*Seitengasse*	
wrinkled	*runzlig*	noun: wrinkle
out of earshot	*außer Hörweite*	

Study vocab "Songs and singers"

Talking about music

melody	Melodie	melody = tune
out of tune	verstimmt	My guitar is out of tune.
chord	Akkord	
verse	Vers, Strophe	
chorus	Refrain	
lyrics	Text	I would like to sing along, but I don't know the lyrics.
singer-songwriter	Liedermacher	
(to) release an album/a CD	ein Album/eine CD veröffentlichen	
(to) record a CD	eine CD aufnehmen	

James Taylor: Fire and rain

(to) cause trouble	Schwierigkeiten machen	
(heroin-)addiction	(Heroin-)Sucht	adj.: addicted
(to) graduate from school	einen Schulabschluss machen	
(to) drop out of school	die Schule abbrechen	
rehab	Entziehungskur	"rehab" is short for "rehabilitation"
psychiatric institution	psychiatrische Anstalt	
setback	Rückschlag, Dämpfer	
(to) make a stand	Widerstand leisten	
(to) see sth/sb through sth	jdn./etw. durch etw. begleiten	(to) see sb through = to help sb

Nelly: Ride wit me

Air Force	Luftwaffe	Army = *Heer*; Navy = *Marine*
(to) split up	sich trennen	His parents split up last year.
(to) get divorced	geschieden werden	(to) get divorced ↔ (to) get married
(to) divorce sb	sich von jdm. scheiden lassen	
(to) fit into sth	in etw. hineinpassen	
(to) peep (coll.)	linsen, verstohlen gucken (ugs.)	
snotty (coll.)	hochnäsig, arrogant (ugs.)	
rude	grob; unanständig	
(to) dig sth (coll.)	etw. gut finden (ugs.)	
measurement	Maß	
(to) glare	funkeln, glänzen	

Ben Harper: Burn one down

breakthrough	Durchbruch	
(to) grow up with one's mother	bei seiner Mutter aufwachsen	
(to) perform publicly	öffentlich auftreten	
(to) pass sth over	etw. weiterreichen	
harm	Schaden, Unheil	
(to) cause harm	Schaden anrichten	
herb	Kraut	
gift	Geschenk	gift = present
blessing	Segen	verb: (to) bless sb/sth
curse	Fluch	verb: (to) curse = *(ver)fluchen*

Miscellaneous

charity	Wohltätigkeit	
disabled	behindert	disabled = handicapped
bone marrow	Knochenmark	
cancer	Krebs (Krankheit; Sternzeichen)	
women's rights	Frauenrechte	
environment	Umwelt	

Study vocab part III

Sports
(to) work out	*trainieren*	noun: workout
stationary bicycle	*Heimtrainer*	
treadmill	*Laufband*	
jump rope	*Springseil*	
bead of sweat	*Schweißperle, -tropfen*	
push-up	*Liegestütz*	
chin-up	*Klimmzug*	
muscle	*Muskel*	

In bars and restaurants
bartender	*Barkeeper*	
bar	*Theke*	
waiter	*Kellner*	female: waitress
sip	*kleiner Schluck, Schlückchen*	(to) take a sip = *ein Schlückchen nehmen*
(to) sip at sth	*an etw. nippen*	(to) sip ↔ (to) gulp (= *gierig saufen*)
(to) take a swig	*einen Schluck nehmen*	
(to) order sth	*etw. bestellen*	nound: order
(to) eat	*essen*	
food	*das Essen*	
(to) dine	*dinieren*	(to) dine ↔ (to) wolf down (= *fressen, schlingen*)
(to) relish sth	*etw. genießen*	(to) relish = (to) enjoy, (to) cherish

Out on the sea (and under it)
vessel	*Wasserfahrzeug*	
skiff	*kleines Boot*	a small boat
whale	*Wal*	
whaler	*Walfänger*	
harpoon	*Harpune*	
school of fish	*Fischschwarm*	Sven had to fight a school of sharks.
surface	*Oberfläche*	
sea bottom	*Meeresgrund*	

Movements
(to) beckon sb over	*jdn. zu sich winken*	
(to) flex a muscle	*einen Muskel anspannen*	
(to) fend sb off	*jdn. abwehren*	Sara fends Chris off when he tries to kiss her.
(to) whap sth down	*etw. hinknallen*	
(to) readjust sth	*etw. zurechtziehen, zurechtrücken*	
(to) limp	*humpeln, hinken*	
(to) motion to sb	*jdm. ein Zeichen geben*	
(to) slam	*rammen, schlagen, stoßen*	(to) slam the door

Miscellaneous
out of earshot	*außer Hörweite*	
(to) perturb sb	*jdn. durcheinanderbringen, verwirren*	(to) perturb sb = (to) confuse sb
(to) wreck sth	*etw. demolieren*	noun: wreck = Wrack
wreckage	*die Trümmer*	
(to) sob	*schluchzen, heulen*	
moisture	*Feuchtigkeit*	adj.: moist
startling	*verblüffend*	(to) startle sb = *jdn. verblüffen*; (to) be startled = *verblüfft sein*
(to) exhale	*ausatmen*	(to) exhale ↔ (to) inhale
sandpaper	*Schmirgelpapier*	
pitch black	*pechschwarz*	
(to) line up	*sich in Reih und Glied aufstellen*	
sulfur	*Schwefel*	
wailing	*Klagelaut, Geheul*	verb: (to) wail = *heulen, (weh-)klagen*

Study vocab part IV

Television

TV set	Fernseher, Fernsehgerät	
remote control	Fernbedienung	"remote" = short for remote control
network	(Fernseh-)Sender	
(to) channel-surf	zappen	
muted	lautlos gestellt	
TV series	Fernsehserie	24 is a successful TV series.
episode	Folge (einer Fernsehserie)	
season	Staffel (einer Fernsehserie)	There are 15 episodes in the new season of the series.
rerun	Wiederholung	Last night I watched a rerun episode of 24.

Word field "speaking"

(to) speak	sprechen	
(to) mumble	nuscheln	
(to) murmur	murmeln	
(to) whisper	flüstern	
(to) talk	sich unterhalten	(to) talk = (to) chat
(to) utter sth	etw. äußern, aussprechen	He uttered a threat. = Er sprach eine Drohung aus.
(to) give a speech	eine Rede halten	
(to) yell	schreien	

In a store

cashier	Kassierer(in)	
checkout	Kasse	checkout = register
counter	Ladentheke	
aisle	Gang zwischen Regalen	
shop window	Schaufenster	
(to) trade in sth	mit etw. handeln	
(to) trade sth in	etw. in Zahlung geben	
grocery store	Lebensmittelgeschäft	
toy store	Spielwarenladen	
(to) shoplift	Ladendiebstahl begehen, klauen	noun: shoplifter

Cars

steering wheel	Lenkrad	
(to) steer	lenken	
(to) pull over	rechts ranfahren	
gear	Gang	
gear shift	Gangschaltung	With the gear shift you can shift up and down.
clutch	Kupplung	
windscreen	Windschutzscheibe	
glove compartment	Handschuhfach	
backseat	Rücksitz	
passenger seat	Beifahrersitz	
driver's seat	Fahrersitz	
blinker (AE)	Blinker	blinker (AE) = indicator (BE)
rearview mirror	Rückspiegel	
(to) hail a cab	ein Taxi rufen	

Miscellaneous

(to) restore sth	etw. restaurieren	
sage	weise	noun: sage = der Weise/die Weise
(to) do a cartwheel	ein Rad schlagen	
polar bear	Eisbär	
(to) stroke sth	etw. streicheln	(to) stroke = (to) pet
solemn	feierlich	
report card	Schulzeugnis	report card (AE) = school report (BE)
(to) chuckle	kichern	(to) chuckle = (to) giggle
talkative	gesprächig, mitteilsam	
spark	Funke	
in no time	im Nu	He learned English in no time.

Study vocab part V

Weather

drizzle	*Nieselregen*	verb: (to) drizzle
snowflake	*Schneeflocke*	
snowdrift	*Schneewehe*	
blizzard	*Schneesturm*	
(to) pick up	*auffrischen*	The wind picked up.
gust (of wind)	*Bö*	
hail	*Hagel*	verb: (to) hail
precipitation	*Niederschlag*	
cloudy	*bewölkt*	
thunderstorm	*Gewitter*	
weather forecast	*Wettervorhersage*	
weather-resistant	*wetterfest*	

In the barbershop

barber	*Friseur*	barber = hairdresser
hair (no pl.)	*das Haar, Haare*	
haircut	*Haarschnitt*	
hairstyle	*Frisur*	hairstyle = hairdo
razor	*Rasierer*	
razor blade	*Rasierklinge*	
straight razor	*Rasiermesser*	
electric trimmer	*elektrischer Haarschneider*	
(to) dye one's hair	*sich die Haare färben*	
washbasin	*Waschbecken*	washbasin = sink
tap	*Wasserhahn*	

At a party

(to) party (coll.)	*Party machen (ugs.)*	
guest	*Gast*	
host	*Gastgeber*	
stereo	*Stereoanlage*	
(loud)speaker	*Lautsprecher*	
bar stool	*Barhocker*	
match	*Streichholz*	
matchbox	*Streichholzschachtel*	
a crush of people	*Menschengedränge*	
beverage	*Getränk*	
(to) chug	*auf einen Zug austrinken*	
(to) have a drink	*etw. trinken*	

Miscellaneous

(to) recall sb	*sich an jdn. erinnern*	(to) recall = (to) remember
frantic	*wild, wahnsinnig*	adv.: frantically
(to) be doomed	*dem Untergang geweiht sein*	
hydrogen	*Wasserstoff*	
oxygen	*Sauerstoff*	
protective	*(be-)schützend, fürsorglich*	noun: protection
(to) tire oneself out	*sich verausgaben*	
(to) become distracted	*abgelenkt werden*	verb: (to) distract sb = *jmd. ablenken*
numb	*gefühllos, betäubt*	noun: numbness = *Gefühllosigkeit*
posture	*Körperhaltung*	
stooped	*gebeugt, gebückt*	a stooped posture
(to) stand by sb	*zu jdm. halten*	
slightly ajar	*einen Spalt geöffnet*	The door stood slightly ajar.
keyguard (of a phone)	*Tastensperre (eines Telefons)*	
(to) set the keyguard	*die Tastensperre einschalten*	
hall(way)	*Flur*	
in a row	*nacheinander*	He scored five points in a row.

Component 5

Part III (pp. 97–121) – The action slows down

Im Gegensatz zum klassischen Drama fehlt in *Twelve* die Klimax im dritten Akt. Ganz im Gegenteil: *part III* plätschert eher so vor sich hin und ist mit 24 Seiten auch der kürzeste. Zu Beginn wird nochmals deutlich, wie wichtig die Party für Sara Ludlow ist, die wieder bei Chris ist, um Geld für *Twelve* zu holen, das Jessica für die Party organisieren soll. Molly fragt White Mike um Rat wegen ihrer Verabredung mit Tobias. White Mike muss sich verstellen, da Molly nicht weiß, dass er Drogendealer ist.

Fast die Hälfte von Teil 3 ist Andrew gewidmet, der einen alten Seefahrer kennenlernt und mit ihm in eine Bar geht. Diese Episode hat nichts mit der eigentlichen Handlung zu tun, verdeutlicht jedoch die Gleichgültigkeit der Jugendlichen in *Twelve*. Während sich bei Sara und Molly alles um die unmittelbare Zukunft dreht, sieht sich Andrew mit persönlichen Fragen über seine Zukunft konfrontiert und wird von einem – vom sozialen Status her gesehen – unterprivilegierten Ex-Seefahrer über das Leben und leidenschaftliches Handeln belehrt. Interessant ist auch, dass Claude der Einzige zu sein scheint, der sich leidenschaftlich einer Sache widmet, nämlich seiner Waffensammlung.

Im dritten Teil des *Components* wird White Mike nochmals näher beleuchtet. In Kapitel 45 fühlt er sich sichtlich unwohl, weil er Molly anlügen muss, damit sie nichts von seiner Tätigkeit als Dealer erfährt. In Kapitel 49 muss er in ein dunkles Loch steigen, um eine Tüte Marihuana zu holen. Ist die Ratte dort unten ein Vorbote des Todes?

5.1 It's Sunday in New York City

Der Sonntag plätschert eher gemächlich dahin. Teil 3 besteht nur aus 10 Kapiteln, die vergleichsweise lang sind. So schafft es Nick McDonell, den Rhythmus im Vergleich zu den anderen Teilen zu verlangsamen.

Als Hausaufgabe lesen die Schülerinnen und Schüler Teil 3 und fassen in jeweils ein bis zwei Sätzen zusammen, wie die Figuren ihren Sonntag verbringen.

Read *part III*.
Summarize how Chris, Sara, Molly, White Mike, Andrew, and Claude spend their Sunday. Don't write more than two sentences for each character. Remember to use the present tense for summaries!

Mögliche Lösungen:
Chris: boxing lesson (which he finishes early), is visited by Sara and gives her money for drugs.
Sara: visits Chris, talks him into giving her money for *Twelve*, hints at having sex with him at the party.
Molly: meets White Mike to ask for advice concerning Tobias and the party.
White Mike: is visited by Molly, has to "switch modes" as she doesn't know about him being a dealer, beeper goes off (Sunday also a workday

for him). Goes out to sell some marijuana, one baggie falls into a hole at a construction site.
Andrew: "has nothing to do" and walks around a park, meets an old sailor and plays chess with him; afterwards they go to a bar where Sven tells Andrew about his life.
Claude: practices with a sword. Later, he sharpens it.

Bevor auf die Ereignisse am Sonntag (*part III*) eingegangen wird, soll die Aufmerksamkeit der Schülerinnen und Schüler darauf gelenkt werden, dass Sonntage einen anderen Rhythmus haben als Werktage. Direkt im Anschluss wird die Hausaufgabe in Partnerarbeit verglichen.

Briefly write down what an ideal Sunday is for you.
Tell a partner about it. Together, think about what makes a Sunday different from normal workdays.
Now compare what you've found out about how the characters in *Twelve* spend their Sunday.

Im Unterrichtsgespräch wird jetzt herausgearbeitet, inwieweit sich der Sonntag in *Twelve* romananalytisch von den anderen Tagen unterscheidet.

Sundays are usually slower than the other days of the week. How does Nick McDonell make the Sunday in part III slower than the other days, apart from characters and plot?

Ein Tafelbild zur Ergebnissicherung könnte so aussehen:

Sunday in New York City – the action slows down

Parts I and II are characterized by frequent jumps between different characters and subplots:
→ Most chapters are rather short.
→ There are many chapters in each part (part I: 15, part II: 26).

Part III is set on a Sunday, and the action slows down:
→ The chapters in part III (esp. ch. 43, 46, and 48) are comparatively long.
→ There are only 10 chapters in part III so that the jumps between characters and subplots are less frequent.

Die Tatsache, dass alles etwas ruhiger ist im Roman, kann jetzt zum Anlass genommen werden, eine Art Zwischenresümee zu ziehen. Dies soll – ganz im Geiste des Sonntags – ohne Zwang, Ergebnissicherung und Tafelbild geschehen, sodass es sinnvoll ist, die Lerngruppe aufzufordern, alles Material bis auf das Buch wegzupacken.

Take a minute and think about *Twelve*.
What is good about the novel? What don't you like so much?
Which characters do you like and why? Which ones don't you like?
How do you like the language?
What makes the plot interesting for you?

Component 5: Part III (pp. 97–121) – The action slows down

5.2 What's your passion?

Part III enthält ganz unterschiedliche Antworten auf diese Frage. Sara und Molly sorgen sich um die Silvesterparty, wohingegen Andrew Fragen zu seiner beruflichen Zukunft beantworten muss, der er recht gleichgültig entgegensieht. Diametral entgegengesetzt zu den übrigen Figuren sind Sven und Claude. Der eine blickt auf ein ereignisreiches Leben voller Abenteuer auf See zurück, der andere richtet seine gesamte Aufmerksamkeit nur noch auf seine Waffensammlung.

Zunächst steht das Wort *passion* im Mittelpunkt und die Schülerinnen und Schüler sollen sich Gedanken darüber machen, was sie leidenschaftlich gerne tun. Anschließend stellt sich die Frage, ob Medizin wirklich eine Leidenschaft von Andrew ist.

On p. 113, l. 14 Sven asks Andrew about his passion.
What makes a "passion" different from a "hobby"?
Do you have a passion? If so, draw a sketch of it on a sheet of paper. Now walk around in class and hold the sketch up in front of you. Look at the other sketches and interview some classmates about their passions and let them interview you about yours.

Ein wichtiger Unterschied zwischen *passion* und *hobby* liegt auf der Gefühlsebene: *a passion is a stronger feeling of liking something. You like a hobby, but you are committed to a passion with all your heart.*

Now read Andrew's answer to Sven's question about his passion and comment on it (p. 113, ll. 16 ff.).

Mögliche Antworten:
- At first he doesn't take the question seriously and does not want to think about a serious answer.
- Andrew has to be forced to answer: this might be because he does not really have a passion and is embarrassed to be confronted with this truth.
- Andrew only "thinks" he is interested in medicine, which is not enough for a passion.

Andrew hat offensichtlich Schwierigkeiten mit der Beantwortung, was natürlich die Frage aufwirft, wie die anderen Figuren auf diese Frage reagieren würden. Deshalb sollen nun in arbeitsteiliger Gruppenarbeit Blog-Einträge geschrieben werden, die über eine Begegnung der anderen Figuren aus Teil 3 mit Sven berichten. Im Mittelpunkt steht jeweils Svens Frage nach der *passion* der Figuren.

Imagine you are Chris/Sara/White Mike/Molly or Claude.
You are sitting in front of your computer to write your daily blog entry. You met Sven earlier today and he confronted you with the question: "What's your passion?"
Write a blog entry that tells about your encounter with Sven using all your knowledge about your character.
Make sure that each group member writes down the entry.

Mögliche Lösungen:
Chris: might mention boxing, but the fact that he is too scared to go to a real boxing gym reveals that his "passion" is not very great. Furthermore, he stops working out as soon as Sara enters.

Sara: will most likely not write about passion but about how *weird*, *strange* or *disgusting* Sven was, as she doesn't seem to have any passions besides her beauty and fame. All she is interested in at the moment is her party.

White Mike: is interested in books, but his time of *passion* seems to be over. An interesting part in this context is chapter 13, in which his report card is quoted. Students might need a hint in this direction.

Molly: might be very confused, yet respond honestly. She will probably mention that she is not clear about her passions at all!

Claude: has the most obvious passion, i.e. weapons. He will write about all the different arms he has purchased so far.

Die Ergebnisse werden im Plenum besprochen. Im weiteren Verlauf des Unterrichtsgesprächs wird deutlich gemacht, dass Claude der Einzige ist, der etwas leidenschaftlich gerne tut. Dass dies ausgerechnet (illegale) Waffen sind, ist bezeichnend für die Figuren in *Twelve*.

What are some similarities and differences between the characters you've just worked on?

Das folgende Tafelbild schließt diese Phase ab:

What's your passion, kids?

In *part III*, Sven, who used to be a passionate sailor, confronts Andrew with a question about his passion.

→ His answer is not very convincing: "I think I'm interested in medicine" (p. 113, ll. 21 f.).

What about the other characters in *part III*?

→ **Chris** is without orientation in life.
→ **Sara** is occupied by her vanity.
→ **Molly** tries to be reflective, but is too confused.
→ **White Mike** has lost his passion.
→ **Claude** is the <u>only</u> passionate character as he is fanatic about his collection of weapons. The fact that some of Claude's weapons are illegal is representative of the kids in *Twelve*, since they tend to be or get involved in activities that are dangerous/illegal.

5.3 White Mike's Sunday – "How weird is this?"

White Mike „arbeitet" auch am Sonntag. Zuvor trifft er sich jedoch mit Molly, die nichts davon weiß, dass er Drogendealer ist. Obwohl – oder gerade weil – ihm sehr viel an Molly liegt, muss er sie anlügen, damit sie nichts davon erfährt. Bei diesem Treffen scheint White Mike Zweifel an seiner Tätigkeit zu haben, die er bisher nur wegen der Zusammenarbeit mit Lionel hatte. Außerdem muss er in eine dunkle Baugrube steigen, um ein Tütchen Marihuana zu sichern. Ratten treiben dort ihr Unwesen und Mike scheint weiter verunsichert. Diese ersten Anzeichen von Zweifel werden später extrem verstärkt, wenn White Mike von

Charlies Tod erfährt, und führen letztendlich zum Showdown zwischen White Mike und Lionel, der Claudes Amoklauf auslöst. Die Dunkelheit und die Ratten können als Vorboten für den Tod verstanden werden, zumal in Kapitel 4 Albert Camus' Buch „Die Pest" und die Ratten darin erwähnt werden (S. 19, Z. 9 ff.).

Es ist also wichtig, die Lerngruppe für diese Entwicklung der Hauptfigur des Romans zu sensibilisieren. Dazu vergleichen die Schülerinnen und Schüler zunächst die Mindmap, die sie über White Mike führen, und aktualisieren sie gegebenenfalls. Um möglichst viele Sprechanlässe zu bieten, geschieht dies in einem „Kugellager". Diese Methode ermöglicht es außerdem, dass viele verschiedene Mindmaps miteinander verglichen werden können. In der Mitte des Klassenzimmers werden zwei konzentrische Stuhlkreise aufgestellt. Die Schülerinnen und Schüler im inneren Kreis schauen nach außen, die im äußeren Kreis nach innen. Es sitzen sich immer zwei Personen direkt gegenüber. Nach einer vereinbarten Zeit rückt der äußere Kreis einen Stuhl weiter, sodass sich lauter neue Gesprächskonstellationen ergeben.

Arrange the circles in the classroom according to your teacher`s instructions.
Compare your mind map on White Mike with those of your fellow students.
In the course of the exercise, make sure you talk about all the facts that you have added since the last time you compared the mind maps in class!
Discuss your different versions and add information that you consider important.
After a certain amount of time, your teacher will tell the students of the outer circle to move clockwise so that you will have a new partner.

Im Anschluss wird im Unterrichtsgespräch der Unterschied zwischen "round" und „flat" characters wiederholt (s. *Copy 3*) und festgehalten, warum White Mike als „round" einzustufen ist.

What are the basic differences between round and flat characters in a novel?
What makes White Mike a round character?

Belege, warum White Mike ein "round character" ist:
- White Mike is complex because he is described from many perspectives (cf. Component 3, 3.3: White Mike = linchpin of the plot).
- The reader not only learns about his looks, but also about his thoughts and his past.
- As the reader learns about his past a development becomes clear (e.g. Mike was a good student who lost his ambition after graduation, partly due to his mother's death).

In Partnerarbeit (*Copy 23* und *Copy 23a*) werden jetzt die beiden Kapitel verglichen, in denen sich White Mike wegen seines Jobs als Drogendealer unwohl fühlt. In Kapitel 23 sind Lionel und die neue Droge *Twelve* der Grund. In Kapitel 45 ist es die Tatsache, dass er eine gute Freundin (Molly) anlügen muss, um eine anständige Fassade aufrechtzuerhalten. Beide Kapitel vermitteln eine Atmosphäre des Unbehagens und der inneren Unruhe, die durch die Wortwahl Nick McDonells erzeugt wird.

Die unbehagliche Atmosphäre für White Mike wird noch verstärkt, als er ein Tütchen Marihuana aus seinem Rucksack verliert und in ein Loch steigen muss, um es wiederzuholen. Dort begegnet er einer Ratte. Ratten wurden schon vorher im Zusammenhang mit Camus'

„Die Pest" als Vorboten des Todes erwähnt, sodass jetzt der Begriff des *foreshadowing* eingeführt werden kann. Dies geschieht im Lehrervortrag mit Tafelbild:

> **Foreshadowing**
>
> Foreshadowing is a narrative technique of implying or hinting at what is going to happen.

Im Anschluss sollen die Schülerinnen und Schüler die Vorausdeutung in Kapitel 49 erkennen. Dazu lesen sie den letzten Abschnitt von Kapitel 4 (S. 19, Z. 9 ff.), den letzten Satz von Kapitel 38 (S. 93, Z. 11 f.) und Kapitel 49 in Einzelarbeit.

> With chapters 4 and 38 in mind, how does Nick McDonell imply that something dangerous is going to happen?

Jetzt kann das obige Tafelbild ergänzt werden:

> **Foreshadowing**
>
> Foreshadowing is a narrative technique of implying or hinting at what is going to happen.
>
> - In chapter 49 White Mike must climb into a dark hole to recover a bag of marijuana.
> - Nick McDonell introduced rats as symbols of death in chapter 4 and 38 when White Mike thinks about Albert Camus's „The Plague".
>
> → Thus, the darkness and a rat that crosses White Mike's path in the hole can be understood as a means of foreshadowing death!

White Mike's growing discomfort with his job

Work with a partner.

Partner A

Reread chapter 23 and write down all the words and phrases which show that White Mike doesn't have a good feeling about dealing drugs:

In one sentence, describe the atmosphere in this chapter:

_____

_____

Partner B

Reread chapter 45 and write down all the words and phrases which show that White Mike feels uncomfortable while talking to Molly.

In one sentence, describe the atmosphere in this chapter:

_____

_____

Now present your findings to your partner. Take notes while listening to her/him!

White Mike's growing discomfort with his job (solutions)

Work with a partner.

Partner A

Reread chapter 23 and write down all the words and phrases which show that White Mike doesn't have a good feeling about dealing drugs:

> uneasy, bad news, creepy dude, yellow bloodshot eyes, "the gun is the scariest thing that goes along with making more money," "the words stuck in White Mike's head," "White Mike feels sorry for her"

In one sentence, describe the atmosphere in this chapter:

The overall atmosphere is very nervous: Jessica is nervous because this is her first drug deal and White Mike is nervous because he has to work with Lionel.

Partner B

Reread chapter 45 and write down all the words and phrases which show that White Mike feels uncomfortable while talking to Molly.

> "He has to switch modes," "He hates this," "White Mike tries to keep his face straight."
>
> In order to block questions about his work he says things like: "How about you? Still the smartest girl in school?" and "That's not what you came over to talk about."

In one sentence, describe the atmosphere in this chapter:

It's an atmosphere of uneasiness and discomfort because White Mike does not really want to lie to Molly, but has to in order not to disappoint her.

Now present your findings to your partner. Take notes while listening to her/him!

Component 6

Part IV (pp. 123–172) – Complex relationships

Part IV arbeitet wieder mehr auf den Höhepunkt hin: die große Silvesterparty. Andrew und Molly werden immer nervöser, weil sie normalerweise nicht auf Partys gehen. Jessica hingegen wird immer unruhiger, weil ihr Vorrat an *Twelve* zu Ende ist und sich ihre Gedanken nur noch um die Droge drehen. White Mike hingegen wird immer nachdenklicher. In diesem *Component* werden verschiedene komplexe Beziehungen unter die Lupe genommen. Zum einen die gestörten Eltern-Kind Beziehungen: Sowohl Jessica als auch Hunter und White Mike haben Probleme mit ihren Eltern. Zum anderen geht es darum, wie die verschiedenen Figuren in *Twelve* zueinander stehen. White Mike steht im Zentrum der Figurenkonstellation, die in Abschnitt 6.2 grafisch umgesetzt werden soll. Im Roman kommen sehr viele verschiedene Figuren vor und durch White Mike lassen sich die meisten von ihnen miteinander verbinden. Vorher rücken jedoch noch Timmy und Mark Rothko ins Blickfeld: Die amüsanten *thuglings* sind die letzten Figuren, die in *Twelve* eingeführt werden. Ihre Funktion im Roman ist *comic relief*.

6.1 Strangers: Parents and kids in *Twelve*

Als Hausaufgabe lesen die Schülerinnen und Schüler Teil 4. Außerdem bearbeiten sie **Copy 24** (Lösungen auf **Copy 24a**) und führen die Mindmap über White Mike fort. Wie das Arbeitsblatt besprochen wird, ist wieder davon abhängig, wie viel Zeit die Lehrkraft zur Verfügung hat: Entweder werden die Lösungen im Plenum besprochen oder vorbereitend in Partnerarbeit verglichen.
Bei der Besprechung des Arbeitsblattes sollte näher auf die verschiedenen Charaktere in Teil 4 eingegangen werden, um das Textverständnis zu sichern. Hierbei kann besonders interessant sein:

- Andrew does things he would rather not do just to please Sara.
- White Mike sees a dealer on Coney Island and feels so uncomfortable that he leaves (p. 140, ll. 3 ff.).
- White Mike is looking for directions (p. 140, ll. 14 ff.). Probably also for a direction in his life?
- Hunter's dad was not held responsible for the death of a schoolmate. A teacher was dismissed, but no other action was taken (ch. 69).
- Jessica acts out a talk show and mentions a killing spree (ch. 62). Foreshadowing?
- Molly is angry and nervous because she has never been to a party and doesn't really know how to behave (ch. 74).

In Teil 4 wird das Verhältnis von Jessica zu ihrer Mutter sowie von Hunter zu seinem Vater in Dialogen dargestellt. Außerdem erzählt ein *Flashback* von Mike und seinem Vater. Alle drei Eltern-Kind-Beziehungen sind sehr problematisch. Ein Grund hierfür ist, dass die Eltern die Kinder mit Geld versorgen, sich aber nicht für sie als Persönlichkeiten interessieren. Somit

Looking back at part IV

1. True or false (if false, correct the statement):

	true	false
Andrew is glad he has some marijuana at home which he can bring to the party.		

2. Tick off the correct answers.

Timmy and Mark Rothko
- ☐ are black
- ☐ talk like gangster rappers
- ☐ are customers of White Mike's
- ☐ all of the above
- ☐ none of the above

Sean
- ☐ loves breakfast
- ☐ gets to hospital by train
- ☐ likes Robert DeNiro in "Taxi Driver"
- ☐ all of the above
- ☐ none of the above

3. White Mike gets on the "F Train." Where does he go and what does he do there? Explain in about 50 words.

4. True or false (if false, correct the statement):

	true	false
Hunter's parents talk to him on the phone.		
Hunter's dad was in trouble as a junior in high school.		

5. Tick off the correct answers.

Jessica
- ☐ acts out a talk show with her bears
- ☐ has lunch with her mother
- ☐ wants to get help from a psychiatrist
- ☐ all of the above
- ☐ none of the above

Molly
- ☐ wears contacts
- ☐ has found an outfit for the party
- ☐ throws a tank top out of the window
- ☐ all of the above
- ☐ none of the above

Looking back at part IV (solutions)

1. True or false (if false, correct the statement):

	true	false
Andrew is glad he has some marijuana at home which he can bring to the party. → He doesn't have any. He has to buy some from White Mike!		X

2. Tick off the correct answers.

Timmy and Mark Rothko
- ☐ are black
- ☒ talk like gangster rappers
- ☒ are customers of White Mike's
- ☐ all of the above
- ☐ none of the above

Sean
- ☐ loves breakfast
- ☐ gets to hospital by train
- ☐ likes Robert DeNiro in "Taxi Driver"
- ☐ all of the above
- ☒ none of the above

3. White Mike gets on the "F Train." Where does he go and what does he do there? Explain in about 50 words.

He goes to Coney Island where he walks around aimlessly and watches other people. It is a spontaneous impulse to see something different from Manhattan. Strangely enough, he decides that the neighbourhood is "seedy" and he wants to leave after seeing another dealer.

4. True or false (if false, correct the statement):

	true	false
Hunter's parents talk to him on the phone. → Only his dad talks to him. His mother is already asleep.		X
Hunter's dad was in trouble as a junior in high school.	X	

5. Tick off the correct answers.

Jessica
- ☒ acts out a talk show with her bears
- ☒ has lunch with her mother
- ☐ wants to get help from a psychiatrist
- ☐ all of the above
- ☐ none of the above

Molly
- ☒ wears contacts
- ☐ has found an outfit for the party
- ☒ throws a tank top out of the window
- ☐ all of the above
- ☐ none of the above

entsteht eine entfremdete und gezwungene Atmosphäre während der Gespräche. Die Jugendlichen haben zwar keine materiellen Sorgen, fühlen sich jedoch allein gelassen und nicht verstanden. Diese gestörten Beziehungen sind zentral für das Verständnis des Romans.

Als Einstieg unterhalten sich die Schülerinnen und Schüler mit einem oder mehreren Partnern darüber, was sie an ihren Eltern schätzen/mögen und was nicht. Ob auch im Plenum darüber geredet wird, entscheidet die Lehrkraft je nach Lerngruppe, da es sich um ein sehr privates Thema handelt.

> With a partner, talk about traits that you don't like about your parents and about those you appreciate.
> Discuss different points of view.

Die Schülerinnen und Schüler erarbeiten die Eltern-Kind-Beziehungen des Romans in einem Rollenspiel. Das Besondere ist hierbei, dass sich die Jugendlichen und Eltern in einer Familientherapie befinden und von einem Psychologen aufgefordert werden, ein Schreibgespräch zu führen. Die Rollenkarten auf *Copy 25* helfen den Schülerinnen und Schülern, sich in ihre Figuren hineinzuversetzen und sich auf ihre Rolle vorzubereiten. Die Methode selbst wird mithilfe von *Copy 26*, die als Folie aufgelegt wird, erklärt. Das Schreibgespräch findet in Gruppen statt, an denen jeweils mehrere Vertreter jeder Rolle teilnehmen. Wie oft jede Eltern-Kind-Konstellation gespielt wird, hängt von der Größe der Klasse ab. Zur Einteilung können die Rollenkarten auf verschiedenfarbiges Papier kopiert werden. Auf jedem Plakat sollten entweder oben oder in der Mitte die Namen der Romanfiguren stehen, die miteinander kommunizieren sollen. Während der gesamten Arbeitsphase wird nicht gesprochen. Auch diejenigen, die dieselbe Figur repräsentieren, unterhalten sich nicht. Es gibt keine feste Reihenfolge, in der die *Statements* aufgeschrieben werden. Jeder, der etwas beitragen möchte, kann dies jederzeit tun. Da im Anschluss eine Ausstellung und Besprechung der Schreibgespräche stattfindet, sollte eine Doppelstunde für diese Methode veranschlagt werden.

Nach Ende der vorgegebenen Zeit werden die Schülerinnen und Schüler aufgefordert, wieder aus ihren Rollen zu schlüpfen und die Plakate an die Wand zu hängen. Während der Ausstellung sollte immer ein Vertreter jeder Gruppe beim jeweiligen Plakat bleiben, um Fragen beantworten zu können.

> Now close your eyes for a moment and step out of the role you have just played.
> Stick your poster on a wall.
> Walk around and read the other discussions that were written in class.
> Make sure that one member of each group stays next to the poster to answer questions.

Im Abschlussgespräch wird über die Erfahrungen gesprochen, die die Schülerinnen und Schüler in ihren Rollen und mit der Methode „Schreibgespräch" gemacht haben, bevor die Eltern-Kind-Beziehungen des Romens analysiert werden.

> How did you feel in your role?
> Was the written discussion a useful instrument for the parents and their kids to get a little closer? Can you give reasons?
> What are the main problems the kids and their parents have with each other?

Role card: Jessica

Imagine you are Jessica:
- You and your mother are attending a family therapy session in which a psychologist asks you to have a written discussion.
- Reread chapters 18 and 65.
- Try to imagine how you feel about your mother.
- Write down something that you have always wanted to tell or ask your mother.

Role card: Jessica's mother

Imagine you are Jessica's mother:
- You and Jessica are attending a family therapy session in which a psychologist asks you to have a written discussion.
- Reread chapter 65.
- Try to imagine how you feel about Jessica.
- What are your worries in life?
- You will be confronted with negative statements by your daughter. How will you react?

Role card: Hunter

Imagine you are Hunter:
- You and your father are attending a family therapy session in which a psychologist asks you to have a written discussion.
- Reread chapters 5, 16, and 68.
- Try to imagine how you feel about your father.
- Write down something that you have always wanted to tell or ask your father.

Role card: Hunter's father (Matt McCulloch)

Imagine you are Hunter's father:
- You and Hunter are attending a family therapy session in which a psychologist asks you to have a written discussion.
- Reread chapters 68 and 69.
- Try to imagine how you feel about Hunter.
- What are your worries in life?
- You will be confronted with negative statements by your son. How will you react?

Role card: White Mike

Imagine you are White Mike:
- You and your father are attending a family therapy session in which a psychologist asks you to have a written discussion.
- Reread chapters 17 and 73.
- Try to imagine how you feel about your father.
- Write down something that you have always wanted to tell or ask your father.

Role card: White Mike's father

Imagine you are White Mike's father:
- You and Mike are attending a family therapy session in which a psychologist asks you to have a written discussion.
- Reread chapter 73.
- Try to imagine how you feel about Mike.
- What are your worries in life?
- You will be confronted with negative statements by your son. How will you react?

The kids and their parents – a written discussion

1. Prepare for the upcoming role play according to the instructions on your role card.

2. At _____ you must find all the students that were assigned to your parent/kid (with the same colour). This is the group you will work in now. (There are always several Jessicas discussing with several mothers etc.!)

3. During your therapy session you are asked to have a "written discussion." You communicate only with written words, <u>you are not allowed to speak, not even if you represent the same character!</u>

4. The kids start the discussion with something they have always wanted to tell their mother/father.

5. After one parent has answered, there is no given order in which the statements are to be written.

6. Your discussion will be over after _____ minutes.

7. Now talk about your experiences in your groups and stick your paper on a wall.

8. At _____ everybody has the chance to read the other discussions that were written in class.

Beispiel für eine Ergebnissicherung:

> **The kids and their parents – complicated relationships**
>
> In *part IV*, three complicated relationships between kids and their parents are described:
> - Jessica and her mother
> - Hunter and his father
> - White Mike and his father
>
> → In all of these relationships, the parents have always thought that providing enough money for the kids was enough.
> → The parents did not spend much time with the kids, who were raised by nannies.
> → There is no trust and no affection in these relationships.

6.2 White Mike – the center of the novel

Ziel in diesem Teil ist die Erstellung eines Schaubildes, das die Beziehungen zwischen den Figuren im Roman darstellt. Ein solches Schaubild verdeutlicht auch noch einmal, dass alle Handlungsstränge durch White Mike verbunden sind. Um die Arbeit am Schaubild zu erleichtern, sollte unbedingt eine vorbereitende Hausaufgabe gegeben werden.

> Make a list of all the characters in the novel.
> Divide them into categories (cf. *Copy 10*: White Mike's "customers," his "friends and family" and "others").

Vor der Erstellung der Figurenkonstellation werden noch die zwei letzten Figuren angesprochen, die in Teil 4 eingeführt werden: Timmy und Mark Rothko. Im Großen und Ganzen spielt *Twelve* vor einem sehr negativen Hintergrund. Gewalt, Drogen, dysfunktionale Familien usw. dominieren die Handlung. Um die Leser nicht zu sehr zu deprimieren, führt Nick McDonell diese beiden Figuren ein. Sie tauchen plötzlich in Teil 4 auf und sorgen durch ihr lächerliches Auftreten und Gehabe für *comic relief*. Die Schülerinnen und Schüler beleuchten hier kurz die *thuglings* und überlegen, warum sie Teil des Romans sind. Als Impuls für ein Unterrichtsgespräch dient Kapitel 58, dessen zweiter (und letzter) Satz an die Tafel geschrieben wird.

> "What in the damn shiz fo a niz?" Who says that and why?
> Describe Timmy and Mark.
> What makes them funny?
> Why do you think Nick McDonell put them in the novel?

Ein Tafelbild könnte so aussehen:

> **Comic relief in *Twelve* – the *thuglings***
>
> All in all, *Twelve* is set before a very negative backdrop. The plot is dominated by violence, drugs, unhappiness, etc.
>
> **However:** Timmy and Mark Rothko are funny, because they are white but dress and talk like black gangster rappers.
>
> - They amuse White Mike and the readers (p.140, l. 21: "... his most amusing customers").
> - They offer *comic relief* because the reader gets the chance to smile or even laugh while reading this rather depressing novel.

Die Frage, in welchem Zusammenhang Timmy und Mark Rothko eingeführt wurden, dient als Überleitung für die Erstellung der Figurenkonstellation. Andrew ist hier der entscheidende Faktor. Er muss Marihuana kaufen und kennt keinen Dealer. Er erinnert sich jedoch an zwei Kiffer (*two little potheads*), die mit ihm in der Schule waren, und will sie kontaktieren (vgl. S. 125, Z. 14 ff.).

> Have a look at the list you prepared as a homework. How are Andrew, White Mike and the *thuglings* connected?
>
> Andrew doesn't know where to get marijuana from, so he contacts his former schoolmates Timmy and Mark Rothko who arrange a deal with White Mike for him.

Die Erstellung der Figurenkonstellation erfolgt mit einer Art Gruppenpuzzle. Die Lehrkraft verteilt Kärtchen mit Nummern und Buchstaben. Zuerst finden sich die gleichen Buchstaben in Gruppen („Stammgruppe") zusammen und fangen mit der Grafik an. Wie auf *Copy 27* dargestellt, soll White Mike im Zentrum der Konstellation stehen. In der Legende tragen die Schülerinnen und Schüler ein, welche Symbole sie für die unterschiedlichen Beziehungen verwenden. Nach einer gewissen Zeit arbeiten die Schüler in neuen Gruppen zusammen, die nach den Zahlen eingeteilt sind („Expertengruppen"). Hier werden die bisherigen Ergebnisse verglichen und gute Ideen können „abgeschaut" werden, um sie dann wieder in die Stammgruppen zu tragen. Für die Auswertung gibt es unterschiedliche Varianten:

- Die Gruppen übertragen ihre Grafik auf ein Poster, das an die Wand gehängt wird, danach gibt es eine Abstimmung über die beste und übersichtlichste Darstellung.
- Die Lehrkraft legt *Copy 27a* als Folie auf und es wird im Plenum über verschiedene Alternativen gesprochen.
- Die Lehrkraft teilt *Copy 27a* aus und die Schüler vergleichen zu Hause.

Zentral ist die Erkenntnis/die Bestätigung, dass White Mike im Zentrum des Geschehens steht und dass fast alle Figuren über White Mike in Beziehung gebracht werden können. Außerdem vertiefen die Schülerinnen und Schüler ihre Textkenntnis, da sie jetzt das ganze Buch durchforsten müssen, um eine möglichst vollständige Grafik erstellen zu können.

> Get together in groups according to the letters assigned by your teacher and try to find out how all the characters in *Twelve* are connected.

Use **Copy 27** to draw a diagram that shows all these connections.
Indicate connections with arrows, invent symbols for the different kinds of connections, and draw them into the legend.
Make sure to use an erasable pencil!
When you are done, get into new groups according to your numbers and compare your diagrams.
Finally, go back to your original groups to finish your diagram with the additional information you received from the other groups.

Falls noch Zeit ist, können die Lösungen auch mit einer Figurenkonstellation verglichen werden, die bei Wikipedia zu finden ist (http://de.wikipedia.org/wiki/Nick_McDonell). Dort wurde nicht nur unvollständig und ungenau gearbeitet, es wurden auch reihenweise Namen falsch geschrieben und weitere Fehler gemacht! Es können also sowohl die Fehler besprochen werden als auch das generelle Problem, dass Informationen aus dem Internet nicht immer richtig sein müssen und daher nicht unreflektiert verwendet werden sollten.

In einem abschließenden Unterrichtsgespräch spekulieren die Schülerinnen und Schüler darüber, wie die Handlung weitergehen bzw. enden könnte:

What do you think will happen next?
Will there be some changes in the constellation of characters?
How do you think the novel will end?

Legend:
friends =
family =
acquaintances =
customer =
colleagues =
fight =
kill =
dead =
in love =

(White Mike)

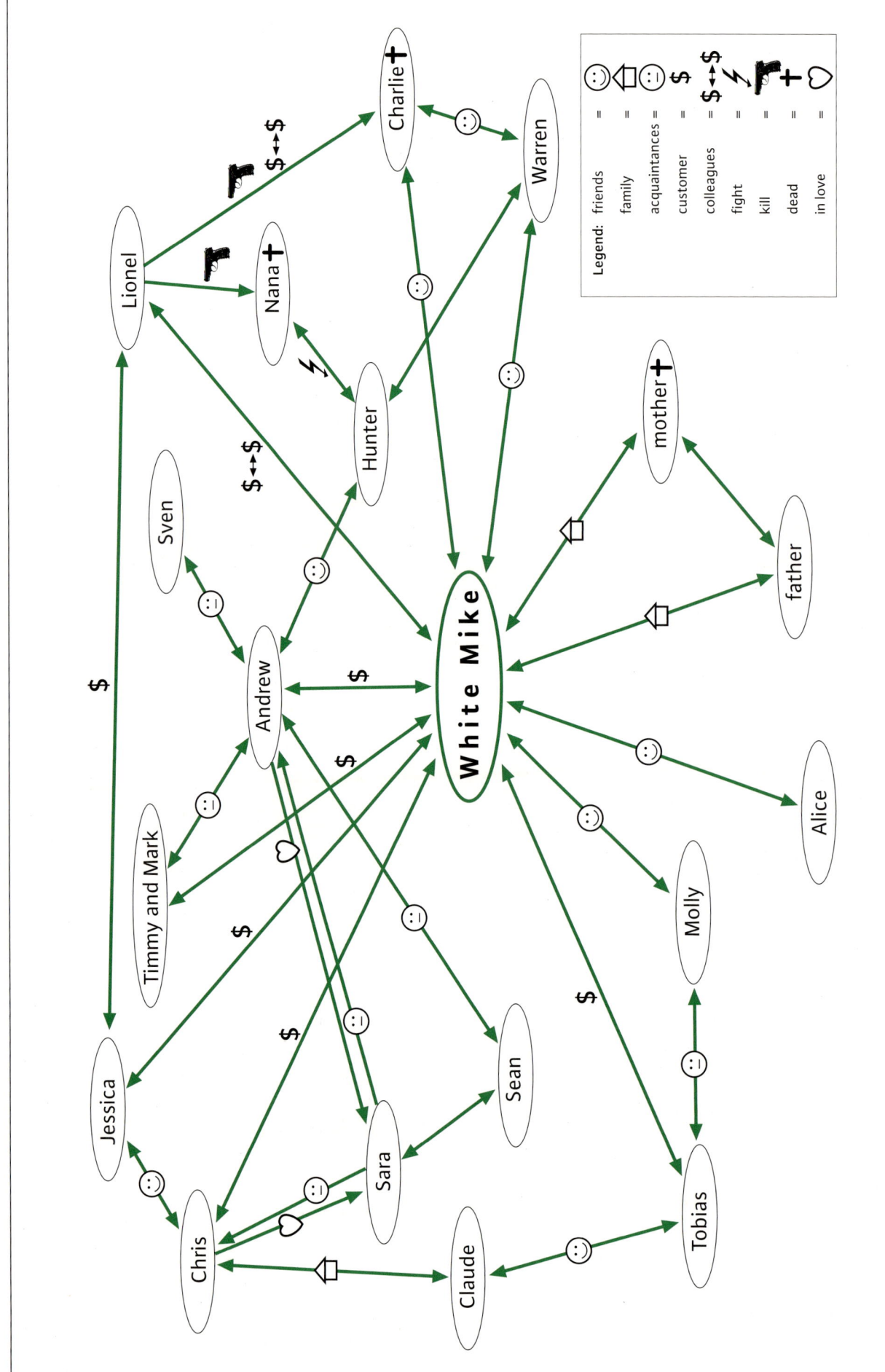

Component 7
Part V (pp. 173–221) and post-reading activities

Der letzte *Component* dieses Unterrichtsmodells beschäftigt sich mit *part V* des Romans, dem *denouement,* und einigen *post-reading activities.* Wenn sich die Handlung auf den Höhepunkt (Silvesterparty) zuspitzt, erinnert die Montage der Kapitel sehr an einen Film. Immer wieder wird zwischen White Mike und anderen Charakteren hin und her geblendet. Somit rückt White Mikes Entwicklung weiter in den Fokus. Mit der Nachricht von Charlies Tod begreift er mehr und mehr, dass er Fehler gemacht hat, und er möchte zur Party gehen, um Jessica und die anderen mit dieser Einsicht zu konfrontieren, womit schließlich die Handlungsstränge zusammengeführt werden. Um die Ähnlichkeit zum Film zu verdeutlichen, sollen die Schülerinnen und Schüler sich überlegen, wie sie einige Kapitel filmisch darstellen würden. Zuvor wird kurz auf einige Grundbegriffe der Filmanalyse eingegangen.

Die erste *post-reading activity* ist das Verfassen einer Charakterisierung von White Mike. Anschließend werden kleine, zunächst eher unbedeutend wirkende Entscheidungen einzelner Charaktere untersucht, die letztendlich zu schwerwiegenden Konsequenzen führen. Dies geschieht vor dem Hintergrund des „Schmetterlingseffektes", den White Mikes Mutter ganz am Anfang des Romans erwähnt.

Der letzte Teil des *Components* liefert Impulse für weitere Aktivitäten, die die Arbeit an *Twelve* ergänzen könnten, jedoch über den Rahmen dieses Unterrichtsmodells hinausgehen würden.

7.1 The party – a massacre

Endlich ist Silvester und die von allen ersehnte Party kommt langsam in Gang. Plötzlich taucht jedoch White Mike auf und rastet völlig aus. Er schlägt Chris ins Gesicht und attackiert Lionel, der daraufhin Charlies Pistole zieht. White Mike erkennt, dass Lionel seinen geliebten Cousin auf dem Gewissen hat, und greift ihn an. Die Schüsse, die Lionel abfeuert, rufen Claude auf den Plan, der unvermittelt und schwer bewaffnet aus seinem Zimmer kommt und die Party zur Katastrophe macht.

Die Schülerinnen und Schüler lesen den letzten Teil des Romans als Hausaufgabe. Dabei richten sie ein besonderes Augenmerk auf White Mikes Entwicklung, indem sie in Stichworten mitschreiben, was er in diesem Teil macht. Da das Massaker sehr unvermittelt geschieht und den Roman abrupt beendet, muss diese Entwicklung genau beobachtet werden, um das Ende verstehen zu können. White Mike beginnt sich nämlich unwohl zu fühlen, als Timmy und Mark Rothko zu ihm nach Hause kommen. Ab dem Zeitpunkt, als er von Charlies Tod erfährt, spielen seine Emotionen verrückt: Er merkt, dass das Drogengeschäft bitterer Ernst ist. Angetrieben von der Einsicht, dass die Lebensweise der Jugendlichen der Upper East Side falsch ist, geht White Mike zu Fuß durch Manhattan. Erst sucht er Zuflucht in einer Kirche, dann jedoch will er etwas unternehmen und geht geradewegs zur Silvesterparty, von der aus er mehrfach angepiepst wurde.

> Read *part V*.
> Make a list of the things White Mike does and write down his moods and emotions. How does he change?

Als Einstieg für die Besprechung der Hausaufgabe überlegen sich die Schülerinnen und Schüler eine alternative Überschrift für Teil 5.

Find an alternative headline for *part V*.
What are the different steps in White Mike's development in this part?
How do his emotions change?

Grafisch kann die Entwicklung so dargestellt werden:

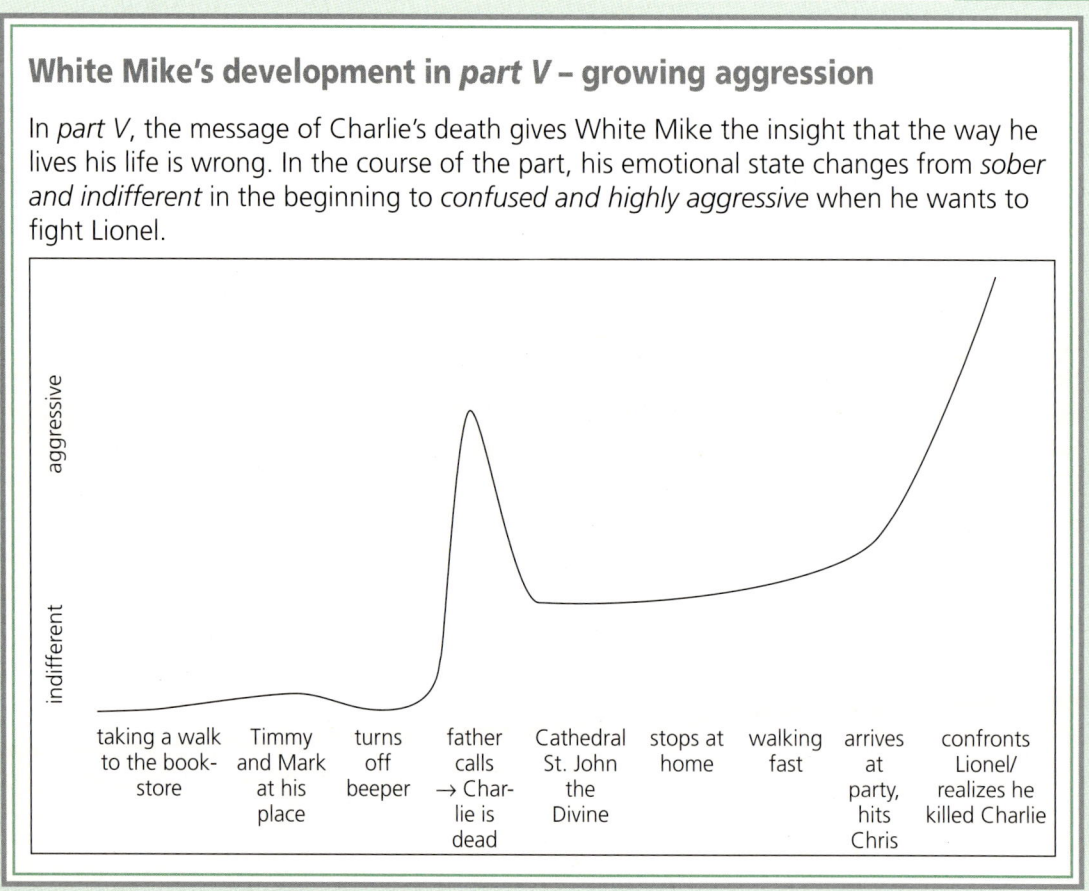

Das brutale und blutrünstige Ende der Party ist für viele Schülerinnen und Schüler schockierend. Deshalb bekommen sie im folgenden Unterrichtsgespräch die Gelegenheit, über ihre Empfindungen zu sprechen, die sie während und nach dem Lesen hatten. Ein sensibler Umgang mit solcherlei Gewaltdarstellungen ist vor dem Hintergrund der Amokläufe, die auch in Deutschland schon stattgefunden haben, wichtig. Eine Diskussion über die Darstellung von Gewalt in den Medien kann sich anschließen.

How did you feel reading the description of the massacre?
Have you read anything like that before?
Do you think such explicit depictions of violence should be banned?
What might be arguments for and against such a ban?

Falls Bedarf besteht und Zeit zur Verfügung steht, kann an dieser Stelle noch tiefer auf die Problematik von Amokläufen eingegangen werden. Die Zusammenhänge zwischen Mediengewalt und solchen Gewaltausbrüchen werden immer kontrovers diskutiert, sodass sich ggf. eine formale Debatte anbietet. Falls die Lehrkraft und die Klasse diese Methode nicht kennen, kann im Plenum oder alternativ auch in Gruppen diskutiert werden.

7.2 Part V – It's like a movie

Filme sind ebenso wie Musik (vgl. *Component 4*) ein zentraler Bestandteil im Leben vieler Schülerinnen und Schüler. Die Tatsache, dass die Anordnung der Kapitel an die Montage eines Films erinnert, macht *Twelve* für sie noch interessanter. Häufig haben die Schülerinnen und Schüler viel Erfahrung mit der Rezeption von Filmen, jedoch nicht mit deren Analyse. Durch die Arbeit mit Teil 5 sollen ihnen Grundlagen und Grundbegriffe der Kameratechnik vermittelt werden, indem sie eine filmische Darstellung von neun Kapiteln planen. In Gruppen werden *frames* der Kapitel beschrieben und skizziert. Sobald die Verfilmung des Romans erhältlich ist, können diese Überlegungen mit der tatsächlichen Realisierung von Regisseur Joel Schumacher verglichen werden. Denkbar ist natürlich auch die Verfilmung einzelner Szenen des Buches durch die Schüler, worauf im Rahmen dieses Unterrichtsmodells aber nicht näher eingegangen werden kann.

Um die Schülerinnen und Schüler für die Verbindung von Film und Roman zu sensibilisieren, wird ihnen zunächst die Parallelmontage der Kapitel 76-78 zu Beginn von Teil 5 bewusst gemacht. Andrew, Molly und Chris wachen jeweils am Beginn eines der Kapitel auf und es wird beschrieben, wie sie den Tag der Party beginnen.

> Read the first sentence of chapters 76, 77 and 78.
> How do these chapters begin?
> As a film director, how would you put these sentences onto the screen?
> Briefly write down your ideas.

> Mögliche Ideen:
> - Have their beds filmed from above and show the characters waking up one after the other.
> - Have only their faces filmed.
> - Have them wake up one after the other within only a few seconds.
> - Have the voices of the characters tell their thoughts immediately after waking up.
> - Use a split screen to show what they are doing at the same time.

Falls die Schülerinnen und Schüler schon Vorerfahrungen haben, kann man genannte Fachbegriffe aufnehmen; ansonsten sollten, vorbereitend für die nächste Gruppenarbeit, Grundbegriffe der Kameratechnik eingeführt werden (*Copy 28* und Tafelbild *Camera angle*). Um nicht zu weit vom eigentlichen Thema abzudriften, beschränkt sich dieses Unterrichtsmodell auf zwei Aspekte der Kameratechnik: Einstellungswinkel (*camera angle*) und Einstellungsgröße (*field size*).

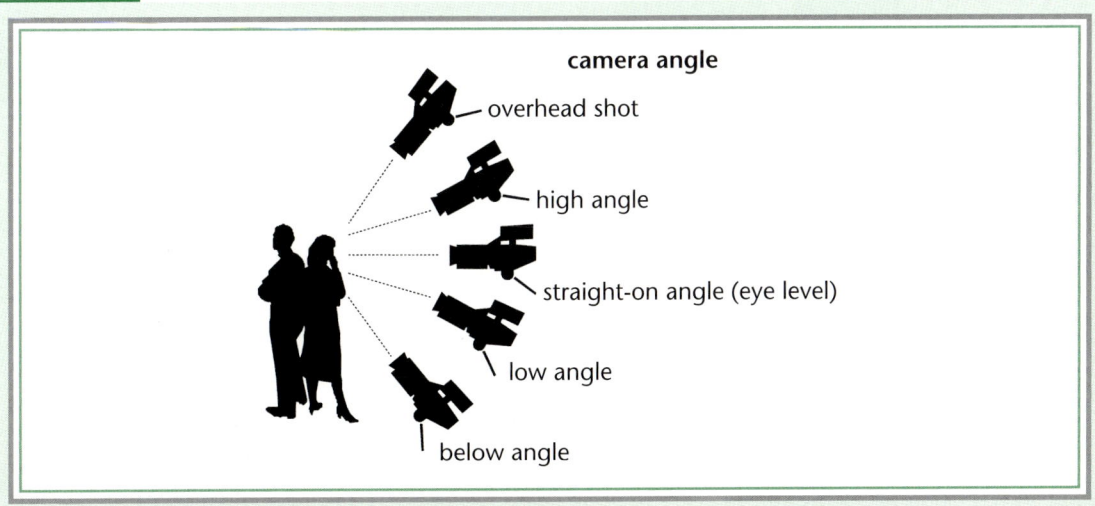

Field sizes

long shot
The camera is at a great distance from the object and shows the entire setting.

medium long shot
The camera shows the object in its surroundings.

full shot
The camera shows the whole object, but little of the surroundings.

medium shot
The camera shows the upper body of a person (down to the waist or hips) or part of an object.

close-up
The camera shows the head and shoulders of a person or is close to an object.

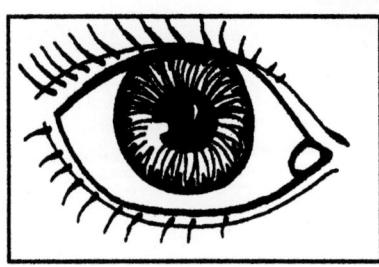

extreme close-up (detail shot)
The camera shows an object (e.g. an eye, a mouth, a knife) in detail. It is very close to the object.

Mit diesem Rüstzeug im Gepäck planen die Schülerinnen und Schüler jetzt die Verfilmung von neun Kapiteln, die die Zeit zwischen der Nachricht von Charlies Tod bis zu White Mikes Ankunft bei der Party beschreiben. Jedes Kapitel wird als eine Szene behandelt und es wird eine Einstellung des Kapitels/der Szene mit den gelernten Begriffen beschrieben und auch skizziert (*Copy 29*).

> Each chapter in part V can be seen as a scene of a film.
> As directors, you are to choose one of the chapters 86–94 to shoot a film.
> Choose the shot you want to make according to its importance for the plot.
> On *Copy 29*, fill out the chart and draw a sketch of your shot in the frame.

Anschließend werden die Skizzen in der richtigen Reihenfolge an die Wand gehängt, damit die Schülerinnen und Schüler den „Film" sehen können. Die Ergebnisse können für alle kopiert oder auch eingescannt und dann digital zur Verfügung gestellt werden.

> While "watching" the scenes, think about why Nick McDonell arranged the chapters the way he did.

Die Lerngruppe erkennt die Sprünge zwischen White Mike und den anderen Charakteren. Diese Sprünge erhöhen die Spannung, da der Zuschauer/Leser wissen möchte, was White Mike tut, nachdem er von Charlies Tod erfahren hat. Außerdem wird beschrieben, was auf der Party passiert, um den Showdown vorzubereiten. Diese Erkenntnis kann so an der Tafel festgehalten werden:

Part V – It's like a movie

In chapters 86–94, the action jumps back and forth between White Mike, Jessica and some other characters at the party.
In between the scenes at the party, White Mike's walk to the party is described.

→ This film-like montage establishes the scene for the showdown at the party.
→ It also inreases tension because the reader is curious about what White Mike is up to after having learned about Charlie's death.

A film scene

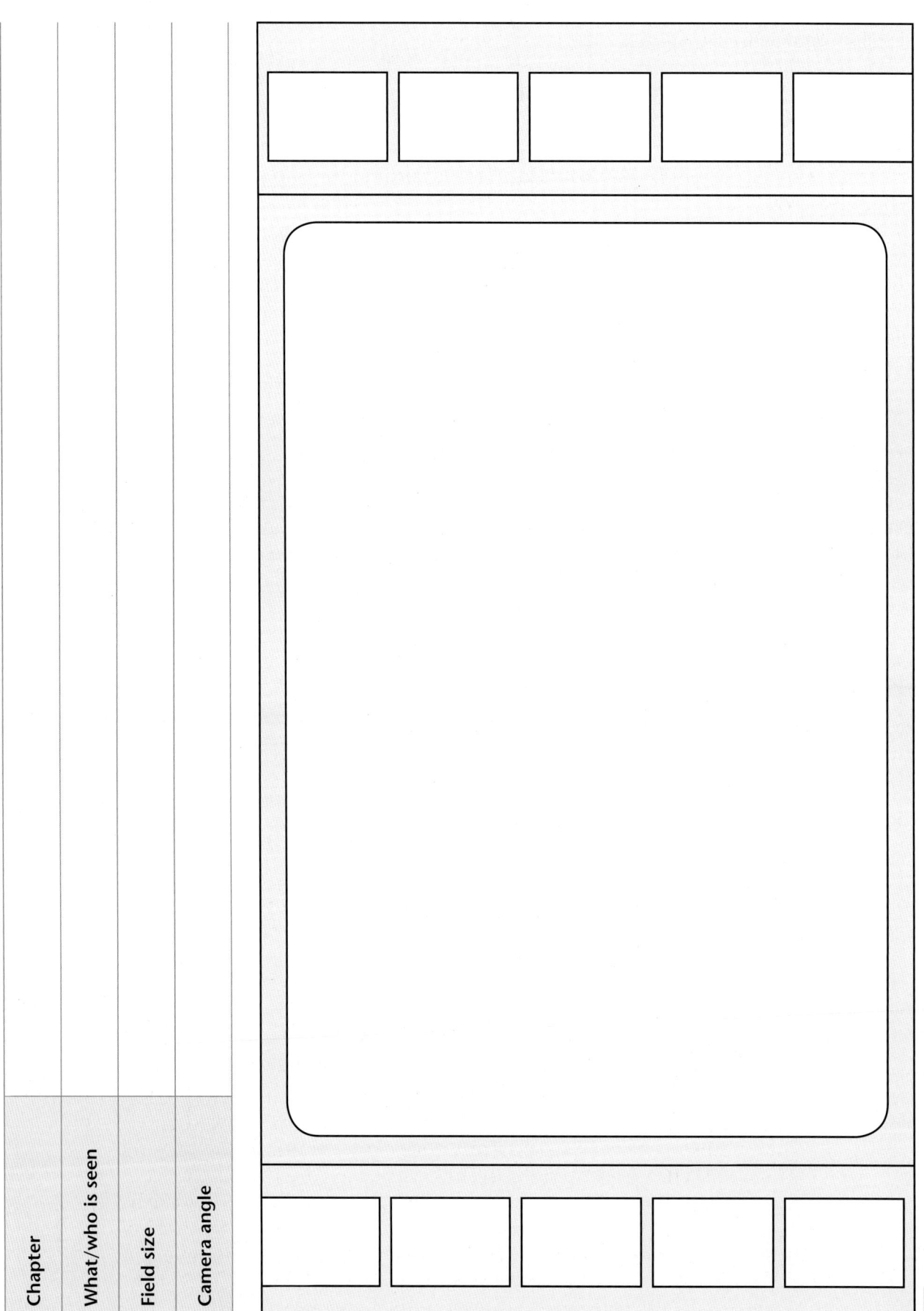

Chapter	What/who is seen	Field size	Camera angle

7.3 White Mike's characterization

Die Charakterisierung einer Figur ist eine klassische Aufgabe der Romananalyse. Hierbei arbeitet der Kurs heraus, wie eine Figur vom Autor porträtiert wird. Bei der Arbeit mit *Twelve* ist eine Charakterisierung der Hauptfigur White Mike sinnvoll, da sich – wie schon mehrfach – alle Handlungsstränge durch ihn verbinden lassen und Nick McDonell diese Figur am ausführlichsten beschreibt. Vorbereitend hat der Kurs in *Component 1* Grundbegriffe der Charakterisierung kennengelernt (s. *Copy 3*, S. 30) und mithilfe der Mind Map ausführliche Informationen über White Mike gesammelt. Diese Informationen werden jetzt gefiltert und in einen zusammenhängenden Text gebracht. Anhand der Beschreibung auf *Copy 30* schreiben die Schülerinnen und Schüler einen ersten Entwurf als Hausaufgabe. Dabei muss unbedingt klar sein, dass nicht alle Informationen verarbeitet werden können und müssen. Somit kommt dem ersten Arbeitsschritt (Markieren wesentlicher Informationen) eine große Bedeutung zu.

> Write a characterization of White Mike according to the instructions on *Copy 30*.

Die Besprechung der Hausaufgabe erfolgt in Gruppen. Zunächst werden die verschiedenen Lösungen verglichen und diskutiert. Am Ende der Phase soll jede Gruppe eine *master version* vorstellen, die gemeinsam erarbeitet wurde. Leistungsstarke Schülerinnen und Schüler erhalten die Möglichkeit, Verantwortung zu übernehmen, leistungsschwächere können davon profitieren, sich aber auch einbringen. Die Gruppen müssen unbedingt dazu angehalten werden, englisch zu sprechen und den Text direkt in englischer Sprache zu verfassen.

> Compare your homework in groups.
> First compare the information you have highlighted on your mind maps and discuss their relevance.
> In a second step, come up with one "master version" in your group.
> Make sure that each group member writes down the text in her/his exercise book.
> Read out the "master version" in class.

Die hier abgedruckte Charakterisierung wäre eine Möglichkeit, die Aufgabe zu bearbeiten:

> White Mike is the main character in Nick McDonell's *Twelve* which was published in 2002. White Mike is taking a year off after high school and spends his time dealing drugs in the Upper East Side of Manhattan. He is the character the reader learns most about, because the author gives a lot of information about him in flashbacks which are printed in italics. On top of that, White Mike is the one character that appears in all the different subplots of the book and finally brings them all together. Still, he is at times a mysterious character. His growing insight about the superficial lives he and all the kids in the Upper East Side are leading finally triggers a terrible massacre at the end of the novel.
> "White Mike is thin and pale like smoke" (p. 5, l. 4). In the very first sentence, White Mike's looks are described. Furthermore, the reader learns that he wears jeans and an overcoat over a hooded sweatshirt (p. 5, l. 5 ff.). White Mike considers himself good-looking, so that girls often stare at him (p. 141, ll. 5 ff.). He is very intelligent and was a good student, as his report card documents in one of the flashbacks (pp. 45 ff.). This same report card also shows that he is very headstrong and does

not want to live up to the educational ideals his teachers consider possible for him.

This idiosyncratic and somewhat strange behaviour is underlined by the fact that he, despite being a very good drug dealer, has never taken any illegal drugs before. Neither has he drunk any alcohol or smoked a cigarette in his life (p. 5, ll. 8ff.). This fact also makes his friends curious about him and they bring up the issue from time to time (e.g. Hunter on p. 74, ll. 6ff. or Alice on pp. 92 and 97).

With regard to his family, he has no siblings and lives with his father, because his mother died three and a half years earlier (p. 61, ll. 12ff.). His father has no time whatsoever for Mike because he is occupied with the restaurants he runs and his new girlfriend. According to some anecdotes told in the book, White Mike had a good and close relationship to his mother. In fact, his mother is the only parent in the book who tries to take part in her child's life and talks to her son about what matters in life (e.g. the talk about chaos theory on pp. 9f.; "Did you hear me Michael? Always live the best life you can" (p. 70, ll. 9f.)). She also mattered to Charlie, White Mike's cousin. She could make him do anything (p. 139, ll. 22ff.).

Charlie was the one who introduced White Mike to drug dealing. He and White Mike were very close friends, and it is when White Mike learns about Charlie's death that he loses control for the first time and finally realizes how dangerous and bad the drug business really is. This insight is a development that starts when he sells "Twelve," a new and dangerous designer drug, to Jessica who is very naïve and insecure during the deal. Furthermore, there is another dealer called Lionel involved here who is the only person who scares him (pp. 66ff). More steps in this development are a conversation with Molly, his only friend who does not know about his job (pp. 104ff.), and his deal with Andrew, whom he warns that buying drugs, especially for someone else, is a bad thing to do (pp. 164ff.).

Finally he wants to take a stand against the rich and spoiled kids' lives and crashes a party to save Jessica from Lionel, the other dealer mentioned above. When he realizes that it was Lionel who killed his beloved cousin, he freaks out and Lionel fires a gun. The gunfire, which leaves Mike wounded, makes another kid draw a weapon and shoot eight kids at the party.

In conclusion, White Mike is the roundest character in the novel and undergoes a thorough development. However, he always remains an odd character who is hard to fathom, which is underlined by his afterword in which he reveals that he has started a new life in Paris and is actually smoking marijuana himself now (pp. 223ff.).

White Mike's characterization

In a characterization, you are supposed to analyze how the author portrays a certain character of a novel. A character's social position, situation, outward appearance, behaviour, words, thoughts, feelings and attitudes are aspects of such a characterization. They work together to give readers or audiences a full and complex picture of the character. Other characters can also play a role in the characterization.

Now you will analyse White Mike as a character and write a characterization about him. Below there are some points to pay attention to while working on the text.

1. Before writing:

- Take your mind map on White Mike and highlight the information you consider most important in each category.
- Order each category – and the highlighted information in the categories – according to importance.

2. While writing:

- Write a short introduction in which you give the name of the novel and the author. Next, present White Mike and his situation.
- In your main part you should organize your notes in paragraphs. Make sure that each paragraph deals with one character trait. **Present the evidence** taken from the text and comment on it. Don't forget to give references to the text (pages and lines).
- Some of the adjectives on **Copy 5** might be useful for your characterization!
- Try to show how the different character traits might **relate** to one another.
- Write a **conclusion** that sums up the results of your analysis.

3. After writing:

- Does your introduction properly set the stage for your analysis of the character?
- Have you analysed all the character traits that you wanted to?
- Is there one paragraph for each character trait?
- Have you linked the different aspects in a logical way?
- Does your conclusion offer a short and convincing summary of your findings?

Component 7: Part V (pp. 173–221) and post-reading activities

7.4 The butterfly effect and *Twelve*

„Was wäre, wenn …" – diese Frage stellt man sich oft, besonders nachdem etwas Schlimmes passiert ist. Schon früh wird das Phänomen von Ursache und Wirkung in *Twelve* thematisiert: Gleich im ersten Kapitel erinnert sich White Mike, wie seine Mutter ihm vom „Schmetterlingseffekt" erzählte. Diese Theorie besagt, dass vermeintlich unbedeutende kleine Veränderungen oder Entscheidungen später tiefgreifende Folgen haben können. Um das Bewusstsein für Ketten von Ursache und Wirkung zu schärfen, sollen sich die Schülerinnen und Schüler zunächst überlegen, welche Ursachen und Entscheidungen letztendlich dazu geführt haben könnten, dass sie ihren besten Freund/ihre beste Freundin oder ihren Freund/ihre Freundin möglicherweise nie getroffen hätten. Vielleicht gibt es auch eine interessante Kette von Ursache und Wirkung im Leben der Lehrkraft, die als Beispiel erzählt werden kann.

> Sometimes minor events or decisions have large consequences.
> Think about your best friend or your boyfriend/girlfriend.
> Which decisions in both your lives could have been made differently so that you probably never would have met?
> This is about your own decisions as well as decisions made by other people, e.g. your parents.
> This chain of events might as well go back until the time your parents met!
> Write down a chain of cause and effect.

Anschließend stellt jeder seine/ihre Kette mindestens zwei anderen Schülerinnen/Schülern vor. Dazu stehen alle auf und bewegen sich frei im Raum.

Um Ursachen und Wirkungen in *Twelve* zu untersuchen, müssen sich die Schülerinnen und Schüler noch einmal mit dem ganzen Roman beschäftigen. Auf *Copy 31* sind Entscheidungen aufgelistet, die letztendlich zum Tod einiger Menschen geführt haben. Es wird in Partnerarbeit gearbeitet, die Lösungen werden im Plenum besprochen.

Lösungsvorschläge für *Copy 31*:

1. If Nana had arrived home later, he wouldn't have witnessed Lionel killing Charlie and would still be alive. So Hunter wouldn't have been arrested and more likely than not he would have appeared at the New Year's Eve party …
2. If Andrew hadn't gone ice-skating alone, he wouldn't have been hospitalized. So he wouldn't have met Sara and wouldn't have lent her the CD. He wouldn't have been invited to the party by Sara and probably wouldn't have gone there and wouldn't have been killed!
3. Charlie finds out that you can buy weapons in the pawn shop where he pawned his mother's necklace. If he hadn't bought a gun, he wouldn't have pulled it against Lionel and probably wouldn't have been killed.
4. If Tobias hadn't been at the beach when he was 11, he wouldn't have been at the agency where he met Molly. So he wouldn't have asked Molly to be his date at the party and Molly wouldn't have gone there and would still be alive.
5. Jessica wouldn't have taken Twelve. She wouldn't have offered herself to Lionel at the party. Probably Lionel wouldn't have shown up in the first place, so that the gunfire that finally brings out Claude from his room wouldn't have happened.

Cause and effect – the butterfly effect in *Twelve*

The story she told him was about how if a butterfly died over a field in Brazil and fell to the ground and made a mouse move or a tiny shoot of grass bend, then everything might be different here, thousands and thousands of miles away.
5 "How come?" he asked.
"Well, if one thing happens and changes something else, then that thing changes something else, right? And that change could come all the way around the world, right here to you in your bed." She tweaked his nose. "Did a butterfly
10 do that?" "Did the butterfly die?" he asked her back.

Nick McDonell, *Twelve*, pp. 9f.

The phenomenon explained by White Mike's mother in this passage is known as the *butterfly effect,* which says that minor changes in a system can ultimately lead to major effects. If you take a closer look at the book, this passage is in the very beginning of the novel for a reason: Many people in the book make minor decisions or do supposedly unimportant things that finally, as the beginning of a chain of cause and effect, lead to the fatal ending of the book.

Think about the decisions described below and explain, in written form, how minor things end up dramatically for the characters in *Twelve*.

1. **Chapter 2:** Nana leaves the Rec earlier than usual. He would have come back home later if not for the fight. What are the consequences for Nana and Hunter?

2. **End of chapter 18 and chapter 20:** Andrew goes ice-skating although Hunter can't come with him. What if he hadn't gone?

3. **Chapter 28:** Charlie needs money and pawns his mother's necklace. What are the consequences?

4. **Chapter 29–31:** Two teenagers meet randomly in the waiting area of a modelling agency. What are the consequences of Tobias's discovery as a model when he was eleven?

5. **Chapter 10:** What if the boy Jessica is making out with hadn't appeared at Chris's first party?

7.5 More ideas for post-reading activities

Hier einige Anregungen für weitere mögliche *post-reading activities*:

- Verfassen eines Zeitungsartikels über das Massaker
- Vergleich verschiedener Buchcover: Welches passt am besten?
- Einzelne Szenen des Filmes könnten von der Klasse verfilmt werden.
- Schreiben einer Buchkritik
- Entwerfen von Merchandise-Artikeln, die den Verkauf des Buches fördern sollen
- Erstellung eines „Tabu"-Spiels, bei dem die Schülerinnen und Schüler Charaktere beschreiben müssen, ohne bestimmte Schlüsselwörter benützen zu dürfen
- Analyse der Debatte „gun rights vs. gun control" in Amerika (auch in Verbindung mit „Bowling for Columbine")

Further reading

1. Literaturhinweise

- McDonell, Nick: *Twelve*, Reclam, Stuttgart 2005
- McDonell, Nick: *The Third Brother*, Antlantic Books, London 2005
- McDonell, Nick: *An Expensive Education*, Antlantic Books, London 2009

2. Internetadressen

Zu Nick McDonell allgemein
- http://www.groveatlantic.com

Privatschulen und – colleges
- http://www.hotchkiss.org
- http://www.andover.edu
- http://www.deerfield.edu

Drogenproblematik
- http://teens.drugabuse.gov/

Sänger und Lieder
- http://www.nelly.net
- http://en.wikipedia.org/wiki/Nelly
- http://www.benharper.com
- http://en.wikipedia.org/wiki/Ben_Harper
- http://www.jamestalyor.com
- http://en.wikipedia.org/wiki/James_Taylor

Bildnachweis

S. 14: Ulf Andersen/Getty Images – S. 33: © Jochen Tack – S. 41: © Falk Verlag, D-73751 Ostfildern – S. 53, o.: © picture-alliance/dpa, m.: action press/Matthias Braun, u.: © Liesa Johannssen/photothek.net – S. 57, 59: © picture-alliance/Jazz Archiv – S. 58: action press/REX FEATURES LTD. – Grafiken: S. 87, 88: © Franz Domke; S. 91, 92: Victor Prischtt

Sollte trotz aller Bemühungen um korrekte Urheberangaben ein Irrtum unterlaufen sein, bitten wir darum, sich mit dem Verlag in Verbindung zu setzen, damit wir eventuell erforderliche Korrekturen vornehmen können.